JENNIFER GRAY

ATTICUS CLAW

Hears a Roar

FABER & FABER

First published in 2016
by Faber and Faber Limited
Bloomsbury House, 74–77 Great Russell Street,
London WC1B 3DA

Designed and typeset by Crow Books
Printed in England by CPI Group (UK) Ltd, Croydon, CR0 4YY

A CIP record for this book
is available from the British Library

ISBN 978–0–571-32178-0

FSC
www.fsc.org
MIX
Paper from
responsible sources
FSC® C101712

2 4 6 8 10 9 7 5 3 1

To Henry – the world's greatest cat

Part One
Littleton-on-Sea

Atticus Grammaticus Cattypuss Claw, once the world's best cat burglar and now its greatest cat detective was on police-catting duty with the kittens at the Littleton-on-Sea Home for Abandoned Cats. They were turning out the attic. It wasn't the most exciting police-catting job Atticus had ever had. In fact, it was probably the most boring one, except for litter picking at the beach. But Atticus had learnt from experience that even the dullest of activities could turn into an adventure, so he went about it with gusto. Besides, he was there to set a good example to the kittens and help them stay out of mischief.

'Come on, everyone, put your paws into it,' he meowed. 'We've nearly finished.'

The kittens were covered with dust. Some of them had cobwebs on their whiskers. The Littleton-on-Sea Home for Abandoned Cats was run by a very old lady called Nellie Smellie. It was actually just *her* home, full of stray cats, and it was a very long time since anyone had tidied the attic. The place was crammed with junk, which was a good thing really as the whole point of tidying it up was to find stuff to sell at the Bigsworth car boot sale later that afternoon, and raise money for the abandoned cats to go on holiday.

Atticus and the kittens had had a successful morning. They had unearthed boxes of books, various lamps, some odd pieces of cutlery, an ancient record player, a plastic loo seat (still in its packaging), several pairs of curtains and a doll's pram, all of which they could sell. They had also discovered a great quantity of wool, together with an even greater quantity of knitting needles and a large number of pattern books, all of which they couldn't.

The reason for this was that Nellie Smellie liked knitting almost as much as she liked cats. She could knit anything from egg cosies to trouser suits. She could knit gloves, hats, scarves, shawls, knickers, slippers, onesies and tights. She could knit blankets, burkas, baby clothes, leg warmers, ear warmers, nose warmers, jumpers, false beards, false teeth, bicycle-seat covers and lampshades. She could knit balls, budgies, teddy bears, cuddly rabbits, Christmas tree decorations and rag dolls. You name it, Nellie Smellie could knit it. She had even taught some of her abandoned lady cats to knit.

(Atticus had tried it once as part of his police-catting duties but he couldn't get the hang of it. He kept dropping stitches, with the result that the patchwork square he was supposed to be making was more hole than knitting. Nellie Smellie tactfully called it *crochet*, which is basically knitting with holes.)

'Anything else to come down?' Callie Cheddar poked her head through the trapdoor to the attic.

Callie was Atticus's owner, along with her brother, Michael. They lived with their mum and dad at number 2 Blossom Crescent, Littleton-on-Sea, not far from Nellie Smellie's house. Most of the time Atticus enjoyed living with the Cheddar family. Callie, Michael and Mrs Cheddar gave him lots of attention and treats, and made room for him on the sofa when he wanted to lie down (which was most of the time, when he wasn't having adventures or police-catting). Inspector Cheddar still had a lot to learn though. He couldn't seem to grasp the fact that Atticus was the boss and kept trying to tell him what to do.

Atticus took a final tour around the rafters. His eye was drawn to a shaft of light that came through the attic window. It illuminated a small wooden chest double the size of a shoebox, which had previously been concealed under the eaves. Atticus padded over and gave the chest a push. It felt heavy; not as heavy as the boxes of books, but too heavy for even a large tabby cat like Atticus to shift on his own.

'I'll help.' One of the kittens joined him. It was Thomas. Atticus knew he shouldn't have favourites, but since he'd started working with the kittens he'd come to like Thomas a lot. Thomas was a tabby, like Atticus, and though he didn't have four white paws and a red handkerchief with his name embroidered on it tied around his neck, or a chewed ear for that matter, even so Thomas reminded Atticus of himself when he was younger. The two of them were both orphans and they both enjoyed getting into mischief. Luckily for Thomas, *he* hadn't been brought up to become a cat burglar like Atticus had.

'Thanks, Thomas,' he said. 'You push, I'll pull.' Between them the two cats heaved the chest along the rafters towards the trapdoor.

Callie reached up and took it from them. She handed it down to Michael, who was holding the ladder.

'This looks interesting,' he said, wiping away the worst of the dust with his sleeve. 'I wonder what's in it.'

Several furry faces peered down from the attic, including one belonging to Atticus. The chest was covered with carvings of animals. Atticus could make out a cat and a bird, a crocodile and some fish. It looked as if it could be even older than Nellie Smellie.

It was while he was peering down at the chest that Atticus started to get a funny tingly feeling in his tail. Gradually it spread all the way through his fur, along his body to the tips of his ears. He'd had that feeling before. His best friend Mimi, the pretty Burmese, called it instinct. It was a sort of sixth sense cats had along with the other five normal ones. It warned him when danger was close.

'Maybe we could sell it at the car boot sale,' said Callie.

No! thought Atticus. *Put it back!*

'Let's have a look inside,' said Michael.

No! thought Atticus. *Don't open it!*

Michael lifted the lid.

Atticus started. A horrible skull-like face stared back at him. It seemed neither human nor animal. The face was shaped like a man's and was fringed all around with feathers. The eye sockets were empty and in place of a nose it had a long, curved beak.

Some of the kittens began to whimper. They all hid behind Atticus, apart from Thomas, who was so engrossed in the grizzly spectacle that he nearly fell out of the attic. Atticus caught him by the tail just in time.

'It's a mask,' Michael said. 'There's another one underneath it.' He picked up the feathered face carefully.

The second mask was even more horrible than the first. It was the distorted face of a great, snarling, black-spotted cat.

'What is it?' asked Callie. 'Or rather, what *was* it?'

'A leopard, I think,' Michael said. 'Or a jaguar.'

Atticus's good ear drooped. He'd seen pictures of leopards and jaguars on the TV. They were beautiful animals: like him really, except they were much bigger and had spots instead of stripes. And they lived in the jungle, not in Littleton-on-Sea, and ate other animals, not cat food. He wondered what sort of a human would want to wear a dead cat on their face.

'Is there anything else?' Callie asked her brother.

Michael removed the masks carefully. 'There's a journal,' he said.

Atticus risked another look. At the bottom of the chest was an old exercise book with lots of loose pages stuffed inside. The yellowing contents were bound together with frayed string. Written across the front in bold handwriting were the words:

In Search of the
Lost Treasure of the Jaguar Gods

By Howard Toffly
1897

'Howard Toffly!' Callie whispered. She looked up. 'Oh, Atticus, you are clever!'

Atticus's earlier sense of foreboding was replaced by a feeling of excitement. Howard Toffly was a famous explorer who had once lived in Littleton-on-Sea. The chest must be important if it had belonged to him, even if its contents were rather mysterious.

Atticus purred loudly. He didn't mind that.

In fact Atticus loved a good mystery, especially when he was in the middle of it!

Atticus and the children hurried outside with the kittens to show the others. Mrs Cheddar was sorting through the junk in the front garden, while Inspector Cheddar went round with a measuring tape to see if it would fit into the car boot. Inspector Cheddar called it 'taking charge', Atticus called it 'being lazy' – the Inspector always seemed to find some way of getting out of the hard work.

Just then a motorbike roared up outside the house. It was Atticus's old friend, Mrs Tucker.

'I thought I'd come and give you a hand,' Mrs Tucker said, stepping off the bike and removing her helmet. Mrs Tucker was the children's childminder. She had once been a secret agent, code named Whelk.

'Where's Mr Tucker?' asked Callie.

'He's out fishing with Bones.'

Mr Tucker was a fisherman. He had a wooden leg and was the proud owner of the world's bushiest beard-jumper, which was a sort of beard and jumper mixed up in one big hairy tangle. Bones was his ship's cat.

Atticus purred a greeting. He was very fond of the Tuckers, and they were very fond of him. Before his arrival in Littleton-on-Sea they had lived in a tiny cottage by the sea. Thanks to Atticus they had discovered they were rich and now they lived in the same stately home Howard Toffly had once lived in – Toffly Hall. Being rich hadn't changed them though. Mrs Tucker still helped out with the children and gave Atticus sardines from her basket. And Mr Tucker still allowed Atticus to pick bits of food out of his beard-jumper when Mrs Tucker wasn't looking. Unlike Inspector Cheddar, they both understood cats.

'What have you got there?' Mrs Tucker took the chest from Michael. Atticus was interested to see that she was wearing a new tank top with the words 'Never Fear, Edna's Here' emblazoned across the front. Nellie Smellie must have knitted it for her, he supposed.

'We're not sure.' Callie opened the lid to let her see. 'Atticus found it in the attic.'

Mrs Tucker took out the masks one at a time, then the journal. 'In Search of the Lost Treasure of the Jaguar Gods.' She read the title out loud and whistled. 'I wonder how this lot got into Nellie's attic?' she said, puzzled.

'There's Nellie,' Michael said. 'Let's ask her.'

Nellie Smellie hobbled towards them carrying a tea tray laden with cups, saucers, a teapot and an old biscuit tin.

Atticus regarded her curiously with his big green eyes. She was dressed in a long black skirt, mildewed white blouse and green cardigan with holes in the elbows. A knitted purple shawl hung around her scrawny shoulders, and her long white hair was pinned up in a scraggy bun. Atticus wondered how old she actually was. Probably about five hundred in cat years, he decided. It struck him for the first time that if she wasn't just a batty

13

old cat lady who liked knitting, anyone might have thought she was a witch!

'Atticus found these in the attic.' Michael held up the masks to show Nellie. 'They belonged to Howard Toffly.'

'They were with this.' Callie offered her the journal. 'Do you know how they got there?'

Nellie's wizened hands started to shake. The teacups rattled dangerously.

Atticus wondered what was wrong. Nellie wasn't normally shaky, or she'd never be able to do any knitting. He watched anxiously as she set the tea things down on a picnic table, sank into a deckchair and fanned herself with the tray.

'Howard Toffly gave me the chest to look after when I was working as a chambermaid at Toffly Hall,' Nellie said by way of explanation. 'He brought it back from one of his early expeditions to the jungle.' She eyed the masks with distaste and frowned. 'He never said what was in it, mind, or I wouldn't have agreed to take it.'

'Why did he give it to you, though?' Callie insisted. 'Why didn't he keep it in his own attic?'

Nellie shrugged. 'It was after he got cursed by that Egyptian cat pharaoh and took against cats,' she said. 'I suppose he didn't want to have a dead one in the attic.' She let out a cackle. 'Howard Toffly wouldn't have liked *you* much, would he, Atticus?'

Atticus purred modestly. It had turned out that he was distantly related to the Egyptian cat pharaoh in question, but *that* was another story!

'It's just as well Howard Toffly *did* give it to you,' Mrs Tucker commented, 'or his beastly relatives would have found it. They'd have been after the lost treasure of the jaguar gods before you could say "beard-jumper".'

That was true, Atticus thought. The beastly relatives Mrs Tucker was referring to were Lord and Lady Toffly. At precisely the same time the Tuckers had discovered they were rich and moved into Toffly Hall (also thanks to Atticus), the Tofflys had discovered they were poor and had moved to the caravan park where they eked out a living polishing spoons. And in the same way that Mr and Mrs Tucker hadn't changed since they had become rich, the Tofflys hadn't changed since they had become poor, but in the Tuckers' case they were still nice and in the Tofflys' case they were still beastly.

'Hmmmm.' All of a sudden Nellie hopped out of the deckchair, plucked the masks and the journal from the children's grasp, put them back in the chest and banged the lid shut. 'That's better,' she said, wiping her hands on her skirt.

Atticus meowed his agreement. The masks gave him the creeps. He was glad he didn't have to look at them any more. In fact he'd be happy if he never had to see them again. He arched his back and rubbed his whiskers against Nellie's deckchair to show he approved of her actions. Then he let out a deep throaty purr and jumped on to her lap.

'Did Howard Toffly ever say anything to you about the lost treasure, Nellie?' Callie asked.

Nellie shook her head slowly from side to side like a tortoise. 'No. Not a dicky bird. I don't know any more about it than you do.'

'Let's look in the journal,' Michael suggested. 'There's bound to be something about it in there.'

'I wouldn't if I were you!' Nellie Smellie said sharply. Her normally placid face assumed a resolute expression. 'There's a bad vibe coming from that chest. I think it's the masks.' She gave Atticus a meaningful look.

A bad vibe? Atticus blinked back at her. That's what *he'd* thought before he got carried away by the excitement of his discovery. *Nellie Smellie felt it too?* He'd never come across a *human* with instinct before. He must remember to tell Mimi.

'What rot!' Inspector Cheddar bustled over.

'It's not rot,' Nellie Smellie said solemnly. 'It's true. Those masks are very powerful. You shouldn't mess with them.' She stroked Atticus's neck and said in an undertone, 'And I'm not the only one who thinks so, am I?'

At least that's what Atticus thought she said. Nellie spoke so quietly that no one else apart from him seemed to have heard her. He brushed his ears with a paw to make sure they were clean.

'Powerful in what way?' Mrs Cheddar had joined them. She began to pour the tea.

'Wait a minute and I'll tell you.' Nellie Smellie tipped Atticus off her lap and knelt on the grass beside the chest. She closed her eyes and took a deep breath. Then she reached forwards and ran her fingertips over the carvings.

Atticus watched in astonishment. So did everyone else. *What on earth was she doing?*

'They belonged to an ancient civilisation,' Nellie said.

Atticus felt quite alarmed. Nellie's voice had gone all spooky. She sounded as if she were in a trance!

'The priests wore them when they made human sacrifices to the gods.' Suddenly Nellie's eyes pinged open. She withdrew her hands quickly as if the chest had burnt her. Her voice returned to normal. 'I wouldn't touch them with a bargepole if I were you: they'll bring bad luck.'

'But how do you know?' asked Callie.

'Never you mind,' snapped Nellie. 'I just do.'

Atticus was wondering precisely the same thing.

How could Nellie Smellie possibly know all that from running her hands over the carvings on a wooden chest? Unless . . . A most peculiar suspicion was mounting in his mind. It was almost as if someone had popped the idea in there without him noticing, but now he couldn't get rid of it. He stared hard at Nellie. That black skirt and mildewed blouse really were very . . . well . . . *witchy*, not to mention her wrinkled face and crone-like hands. But there was no such thing as witches, *was there*? He really needed to talk to Mimi.

'Human sacrifices!' Inspector Cheddar sniggered. 'Good one, Nellie!'

Nellie gave him a dirty look.

The Inspector didn't notice. He offered the biscuit tin round. 'Anyone for a rock cake?' he asked.

Atticus shook his head. He'd seen tastier-looking rocks.

Inspector Cheddar helped himself to one and took a bite. His face crumpled in agony.

'What's the matter?' asked Mrs Cheddar anxiously.

'I've broken my tooth!' Inspector Cheddar mumbled.

'Nellie told you those masks would bring bad luck, Dad,' said Callie. 'You should have listened.'

'Shall I fetch some of my Old Hag's Cure-All Ointment?' Nellie offered kindly. 'It's very good for toothache.'

Old Hag's Cure-All Ointment? Atticus could hardly believe his ears. Everything about Nellie today seemed to have a *witchy* sort of meaning.

'No thanks!' Inspector Cheddar held his jaw in his hands.

'I'll call the dentist.' Mrs Cheddar took her mobile phone out of her pocket.

'And I'll phone the British Museum,' said Mrs Tucker. 'We'll show everything to Professor Verry-Clever. He'll know what to do.'

Atticus purred his agreement. Professor Verry-Clever was a professor of Ancient History. In fact it was the Professor who had discovered that Atticus was distantly related to the Egyptian cat pharaoh. He was also an expert on Howard Toffly and his expeditions. If anyone knew anything about the lost treasure of the jaguar gods, he would.

'And I'll lock *this* away in the shed where it can't do any more harm.' Nellie got to her feet and picked up the chest. She was surprisingly strong for an old lady, Atticus noticed.

'Come on, everybody.' Mrs Tucker rolled up her sleeves. 'Let's load up the junk. The car boot sale starts in half an hour.'

21

As soon as they had gone, two black-and-white birds took off from a tree in Nellie Smellie's garden and headed off in the direction of the sea.

They made for the pier. Beneath it, perched amongst the old metal beams, was their nest – a scruffy construction of twigs and leaves, which had been the magpies' home for years. The nest was full of all sorts of interesting things that magpies like to collect: shiny things, like foil sweet wrappers and coins and badges and pieces of glass that had been rubbed smooth by the sea. Of course the magpies would have preferred the nest to be full of even shinier things, like sapphires and rubies and diamonds, but since Atticus Claw's arrival in Littleton-on-Sea, they hadn't had much luck with their thieving, especially since he'd become a police cat. In fact it was so long since they'd managed to steal anything sparkly that they had almost given up hope of ever doing so again.

Until now . . .

The two birds fluttered towards the nest. They had expected to find their leader taking his afternoon nap. Instead, he was strutting up and down the beam in a state of fury, making a noise like a pair of castanets.

'CHAKA-CHAKA-CHAKA-CHAKA-CHAKA!'

'What's got into him?' The first magpie was thin with a hooked foot.

'I dunno, Slasher.' The second was fat with a ragged tail. 'Looks like he's had bad news.'

'We'd better go and cheer him up, Thug me old mate,' Slasher said. 'Tell him about the lost treasure of the jaguar gods.'

They landed clumsily on a rickety beam.

Jimmy Magpie stopped chattering when he saw them. He was bigger than they were and had a glossy sheen to his feathers. His wings were tinged with a deep blue and he had an emerald green stripe to his tail. He regarded them with glittering eyes. 'Fancy a kicking, either of you?' he said hopefully.

'Er, no thanks, Jimmy,' said Slasher. 'Me foot's still sore from when you gave me the last one.'

'What about you, Thug?' Jimmy sidled up to him.

'I'd rather not,' Thug said with dignity. 'It'll make my bum wobble.'

'How about a punch in the crop?'

A punch in the crop was even worse than a kicking. It meant you couldn't swallow properly for days. And Thug liked his food, especially worms.

'Nah,' said Thug. 'I'll pass.'

'What's the matter, Boss?' Slasher asked. 'You were in a good mood when we left. What's happened?'

'Chaka-chaka-chaka-chaka-chaka!' Jimmy let out another volley of chattering. 'I'll tell you what's happened. I got this in the pigeon post.' He handed Slasher a letter. His voice dropped to a deathly whisper. 'It's from *her*.'

Thug and Slasher exchanged horrified glances.

'Not *her* her?' Thug said in a hoarse voice.

Jimmy nodded.

'But I thought she was still in the slammer,' said Slasher.

'Apparently not,' Jimmy snapped. 'She's out. Read it.'

'Okay.'

Dear Jimmy,

The good news is I have fully recovered from being flattened by a large pig. The bicycle-pump treatment I received in Her Majesty's Prison for Bad Birds worked wonders. I am now completely inflated and can squawk even louder than I could before. I have also been released early from Her Majesty's Prison for Bad Birds because I am an endangered species. The doctors have sent me to Nicaragua for rehabilitation, where I am currently staying with the Ambassador, Sir Benjamin Posh-Scoundrel.

The bad news (for you anyway) is that as your wife I am entitled to half of everything you own, including your nest under the pier and anything shiny you or your revolting gang may have collected recently. Please send everything asap care of the British Embassy in Managua. I will ask the Ambassador to provide a diplomatic bag for you to put it in. And don't think about not sending it or I'll make you come over here and scrub my poo bucket.

Your nagging wife,
Pam the Parrot

PS Have you hung up that mirror yet?

There was silence for a moment. Thug broke it with a loud burp. 'I'm glad I'm not married to that old bag.' He shuddered. 'I still have nightmares about cleaning her poo bucket.'

'More like *glue* bucket,' said Slasher. Pam's poo was legendary amongst the magpies, in terms of both its volume and its consistency, not to mention its smell. 'It was like scraping toxic barnacles off a rock.'

'I didn't want to marry her!' Jimmy said bitterly. He eyed Thug nastily. 'I seem to remember it was your idea.'

'Nah,' said Thug. 'It definitely wasn't mine. It was Slasher's. He's the one what has all the ideas around here.'

'Shut up, you moron,' Slasher grumbled.

Jimmy regarded Slasher coldly. 'Well?' he said. 'What have you got to say for yourself?'

'Aw, come on, Boss,' Slasher wheedled. 'It could be worse. I mean, look on the bright side. At least she's going to Nicaragua and not coming here.'

'Yeah,' said Thug. 'Thank the crows for that!' He chortled. 'Imagine living somewhere that's named after knickers!' Very unusually an idea occurred to *him*. 'Hey, Boss, do you think she goes around all day with pants on her head?'

'It's not *Knicker*-agua, you idiot,' said Jimmy, 'it's Nicaragua. It's a country in Central America where parrots come from. Managua is the capital city.'

'All right,' said Thug, none the wiser. 'Keep your feathers on.'

Jimmy gave him a peck.

'Why don't you just give her what she wants, Boss?' asked Slasher. 'Then maybe she'll leave us alone.'

'We can't live in half a nest,' said Thug reasonably. 'We'll fall out.'

'We could build another one,' said Slasher. 'Better still, we could steal someone else's. Then we can forget all about Pam and start filling it up with more shiny things.'

'Talking of shiny things, Boss . . .' Thug told Jimmy Magpie about the discovery in Nellie Smellie's attic.

'The lost treasure of the jaguar gods?' Jimmy said. 'Are you sure?'

'Yeah, we saw the book. It

28

belonged to Howard Toffly, that explorer bloke what lived at Toffly Hall.'

Jimmy's expression grew cunning. 'Tell me about the masks,' he said.

'The decapitated cat one was cool,' Slasher said. 'Like Claw, only bigger, and with spots, not stripes.'

'Nice,' said Jimmy, thinking what a lovely mask a decapitated Atticus would make. He imagined wearing it in front of Pam the parrot. It would give her the fright of her life. With any luck she might drop dead off her perch into her bucket and be preserved forever in her own poo. He could even see the epitaph on her gravestone:

IN MEMORY OF
PAM THE PARROT
RIP
(ROT IN POO)

'But the bird one was pretty freaky,' Slasher said. 'It looked like Thug's mum after she got run over by the ice-cream van.'

Thug let out a sob. 'Me poor old mum!'

'That bad, huh?' Jimmy pulled a face. Thug's

mum had never been a pretty sight but she looked even worse as roadkill.

'Yeah, anyway, they're gonna take the whole lot to Professor Verry-Clever at the British Museum.'

'How come?'

'Cos old Smellie Nellie got all het up about the masks,' Slasher replied. 'Said they were used for human sacrifices. She wouldn't even let the kids open the book.'

'She's off her rocker!' Thug muttered.

'You mean Claw and his cronies don't actually *know* where the lost treasure of the jaguar gods is?" Jimmy said. He was sounding more cheerful by the second.

'Nope. Only that it might be somewhere in the jungle,' Slasher replied.

'What about the Tofflys?'

'Nope.'

'Hmmm . . .' Jimmy thought for a moment. 'We need to steal that book before Claw and his pals get the chance give it to Professor Clever-Clogs.

That way *we'll* be the only ones who can find the treasure.'

'Good thinking, Boss,' Slasher said.

'Just don't tell Pam,' Jimmy reminded them, 'or the old bag will want half of that as well. It's our secret, right?'

Thug looked shifty. He liked secrets. 'You can rely on us, Boss,' he said.

The car boot sale was being held in Bigsworth station car park. It was heaving with people all buying and selling junk. Nellie's stuff proved to be very popular. By half past two everything had been sold, except for the cutlery and the loo seat.

Atticus was amazed at how much rubbish humans bought. He hadn't seen anything he wanted at the car boot sale except for a scratching post to sharpen his claws on. And he didn't even need one of those because he preferred to use the back of the sofa. Humans could be very wasteful, he thought piously.

'How much money did we raise?' asked Callie.

'One hundred and thirty-two pounds and fifty pence,' said Mrs Cheddar, counting up the last coins and putting them in a plastic bag. 'Good job, everyone.'

Atticus didn't think it would be enough to send the cats from the cats' home on holiday but it might be enough for a day at the pet spa and a few ice creams.

'I'm hungry,' said Michael.

'Me too,' said Callie. 'Can we go and get something to eat?'

Atticus thought that sounded like an excellent idea. He hadn't had anything to eat since breakfast.

'How about fish and chips?' Mrs Cheddar suggested. 'There's a shop over there.' She pointed to a parade of shops near the station entrance.

'We'll all go,' said Mrs Tucker. 'Come on, kids, I'll treat you and the kittens. You wait here, Atticus, in case anyone else comes.'

Atticus's chewed ear drooped. 'Don't worry,' Mrs Tucker said. 'We'll bring you something back.'

Off they all went to the fish and chip shop. Atticus retreated to the back of the boot and lay down for a nap. He was just about to doze off when a man and a woman approached the car. The man was short and fat with a red face. He was dressed in a scruffy tweed suit. Billowing from his chin was what looked to Atticus very much like a fake beard. The woman was tall and thin. She wore a headscarf drawn low over her face, a long mac, rubber boots and a pair of sunglasses attached to a false nose. The strange couple started rifling through the cutlery in a very suspicious manner.

Atticus watched them through narrowed eyes. *They were robbers!* He flattened his ears and let out a low, throaty growl. The couple didn't seem to hear. They were engrossed in checking out the cutlery.

'Any spoons?' asked the woman in a low voice.

'A few,' said the man.

'Pass them here.' The woman opened her coat pocket.

Oh no, you don't! Atticus sprang forward, hissing.

'Great Scott!' said the man, jumping back. His eyes fell on Atticus's neckerchief. 'I say,' he said, reading the name embroidered upon it. 'It's him!' He turned to the woman. 'Antonia, it's that frightful police cat, Atticus Claw. The one who's responsible for making us poor! I wish I had my shotgun!'

Antonia! Atticus recognised them now. It was the beastly Tofflys!

'You!' spat Lady Toffly. She picked up a knife and fork and held them in her fists. 'Is anyone coming, Roderick?' she asked.

'No.'

'Good. Keep a lookout, will you, while I skin him? He'll make a nice cushion.' She put one knee in the boot.

Atticus gulped. She had him cornered. *Where was everyone?*

''S everything awright?' a slurred voice said.

Atticus breathed a sigh of relief. Inspector Cheddar. He was back just in time!

Lady Toffly dropped the knife and fork. She shuffled backwards out of the car boot.

'There y'are, Atticus!' Inspector Cheddar said, lurching towards him. 'I've been looking for you all over the place. Where's everyone else?' He bashed into Lady Toffly, sending her sprawling amongst the spoons. 'Oops, sorry 'bout that.'

Atticus regarded Inspector Cheddar with dismay. He looked very unsteady on his feet. And something had happened to his right cheek. It had swollen up like a chipmunk's.

Inspector Cheddar sat down in the boot with a

bump. ''S m' tooth,' he said to no one in particular. He opened his mouth and touched his jaw gingerly. 'Had to go to the dentist.' He tapped his head. 'Feeling a bit woozy.'

So that was it, thought Atticus. He had never been to the dentist, but he had once had his teeth cleaned by his enemy, the vet. The vet had given him an injection first so that it wouldn't hurt (or so he said!). Atticus remembered *he'd* felt pretty woozy afterwards.

''S not much junk left, Atticus,' Inspector Cheddar slurred, looking around the boot. ''Cept spoons.' He picked one up and stared at his reflection.

Atticus wished he could tell the Inspector about the Tofflys trying to steal the spoons. Inspector Cheddar didn't seem to have any idea who the strange couple was! Atticus gave a strangled meow and pointed at them with his paw.

Inspector Cheddar was none the wiser. He offered the spoon to Lord Toffly. 'D'you want it?' he asked. ''S only ten pence. All the money is going to the Littleton-on-Sea Home for Abandoned Cats.'

'No thank you,' Lord Toffly sneered. He took Lady Toffly's arm and made to steer her away.

Good riddance! thought Atticus.

'Be like that!' Inspector Cheddar threw the spoon back on to the pile with a clang. "S a pity we didn't bring that ol' chest of Howard Toffly's you found in Nellie's attic,' he remarked to Atticus. 'Might have got a decent price for it.'

Lady Toffly stopped in her tracks. She turned round slowly. 'What old chest would that be?' she asked in a sugary voice.

Atticus started meowing at the top of his voice. *Inspector Cheddar mustn't tell the Tofflys about the lost treasure of the jaguar gods!*

'I can't tell you,' Inspector Cheddar said.

'Why not?' Lady Toffly demanded.

"N case the beastly Tofflys find out about the los' treasure of the jaguar gods.'

Atticus clapped his paw to his forehead. *Honestly?* He tugged at Inspector Cheddar's sleeve with his teeth. He wished Mrs Tucker would hurry up.

'What if we promise not to *tell* the Tofflys?' Lady Toffly said. 'Not that we know them, of course.' She smiled winningly. 'Just think, if *we* found that treasure for you, you could sell it and give all the money to the cats' home!'

That seemed to get Inspector Cheddar thinking. ''S a good idea,' he said.

No it wasn't! Atticus sunk his claws into Inspector Cheddar's hand. 'Oi!' Inspector Cheddar said. ''S naughty.' He pushed Atticus to one side and beckoned the Tofflys closer. 'There's a journal,' he explained. ''S from one of Howard Toffly's early 'speditions to the jungle.'

For goodness' sake! Atticus launched himself at the Inspector. Inspector Cheddar tucked him firmly under his arm while he finished spilling the beans. 'And there are some masks.' Inspector Cheddar squinted at Lady Toffly. 'I hope you don't mind me saying so, but they're even more hideous than you.'

Lady Toffly gritted her horsy teeth. 'I hope you're – er – keeping the chest somewhere *safe*?' she said, giving Atticus a malicious look.

''S in Nellie Shellie's smed,' Inspector Cheddar said. 'I mean Shellie Mellie's sled.' He tried again. 'Make that Smellie Welly's shned.' He shook his head, yawning. 'Whatever. But don't worry, 's locked, so the beastly Tofflys can't steal it. Then tomorrow Mrs Tucker's going to take it to the British Museum and give it to Professor Verry-Clever.' He gave them a little wave and passed out on top of Atticus.

The delicious smell of fish and chips and the mewing of lots of hungry kittens heralded the return of the others.

'Quick, Roderick!' Lady Toffly grabbed her husband by the fake beard. The two of them made off across the station car park.

'Dad!' Callie and Michael hurried over. 'Are you all right?'

'You're squashing Atticus,' Callie said.

'I'm fine.' Inspector Cheddar sat up. 'Couldn't be better. Where am I, by the way?'

Atticus struggled free. He had to warn the humans about the Tofflys!

'Meow, meow, meow!'

'Do you think Atticus is trying to tell us something?' Michael said.

'Meow, meow, meow!'

'I'm not sure,' said Callie.

'Meow, meow, meow!'

'It's a pity he can't talk,' Mrs Cheddar said. 'I've got a feeling he might be.'

'Meow, meow, meow!'

'Maybe he's just hungry,' said Mrs Tucker. She offered him a parcel of fish and chips.

Atticus gave up. Even the brightest humans could be very dim sometimes. He tucked into his fish and chips. There was only one way to stop the Tofflys from stealing Howard Toffly's journal, he decided; and that was to steal it himself.

That night when everyone had gone to bed Atticus let himself out of the cat flap at number 2 Blossom Crescent into the back garden. He made his way round the side of the house to the road. From there he trotted briskly along the pavement until he reached the cats' home. Checking carefully to make sure there was no sign of the Tofflys he darted across the lawn towards the shed.

Atticus withdrew a long kirby grip, which he had borrowed from Callie's dressing table, from the folds of his neckerchief and raised himself up on his back legs. With one front paw he held the shed door handle; with the other he wriggled the kirby grip into the lock and twisted it to and fro.

Click! The shed door creaked open.

'What are you doing?'

Atticus nearly jumped out of his skin. It was Thomas. The kitten was standing right behind him. He must have crept up while he was picking the lock.

'None of your business,' Atticus said gruffly. 'Go back to bed.'

'No,' said Thomas.

No? Atticus felt exasperated. That was the sort of thing *he* would have said when he was a kitten. 'If you must know, I'm trying to stop the Tofflys from stealing Howard Toffly's journal about the lost treasure of the jaguar gods,' he said crossly. 'Inspector Cheddar told them about it at the car boot sale.' He explained briefly what had happened. '*Now* will you go back to bed?'

Thomas shook his head. 'No,' he said stubbornly. 'I want to help.'

'Oh, all right, then!' Atticus didn't have time to argue. 'Get in!'

Thomas scampered into the shed. Atticus followed him inside and shut the door carefully behind them. The shed was almost as cluttered as Nellie Smellie's attic had been. As well as gardening equipment it was bursting with boxes of firewood, bits of old carpet and what looked like several tons of cat litter in large paper sacks. An old broomstick stood in the corner. Atticus tried not to look at it. The more he thought about Nellie and her witchiness, the more it freaked him out.

'It's up there,' said Thomas.

Three shelves ran along one wall of the shed. Howard Toffly's wooden chest was on the middle one, wedged in beside a number of terracotta pots and a bag of compost.

'I'll get it.' Before Atticus could stop him, the kitten had scrambled up the broomstick and jumped lightly on to the shelf.

Atticus was impressed in spite of himself. Thomas was a natural when it came to cat burgling. He watched the kitten edge along the shelf to the chest and raise the lid. Thomas's top half disappeared inside the chest. It reappeared a minute later. The journal was hooked around Thomas's front paw by the string.

'Good work,' Atticus said.

Just then he heard a familiar sound. It was coming from the trees behind the shed.

'Chaka-chaka-chaka-chaka-chaka!'

The magpies! Atticus's hackles rose. He hadn't expected Jimmy and his gang to show up. 'Thomas,' he hissed, 'it's the magpies. You need to get out of sight. Throw me the journal, then close the lid so they don't suspect anything. Hurry!'

'Okay.' Thomas dropped the journal on to a bag of cat litter. He lowered the lid of the chest then slithered down the broomstick and landed on the floor next to Atticus.

Atticus grabbed the string in his teeth and led the way behind the lawnmower. He slid the journal under the grass box and waited.

TAP! TAP! TAP! TAP! TAP! TAP!

The magpies were trying to break in through the window.

'Put your back into it, Thug. We haven't got all night.'

Atticus flattened his ears. It was his old enemy, Jimmy Magpie.

'I don't want to cut my beak.' Thug's plaintive voice drifted down.

'I've got a better idea,' Slasher chattered. 'Get out of the way, Thug.'

SMASH!

A stone hurtled through the window, making a hole just big enough for a magpie to squeeze through. Jimmy appeared first. Then Slasher, then Thug.

'Ow!' yelped Thug. 'Ow, ow, ow, ow, ow!' His rear end was bigger than the others'. Several black-and-white feathers floated to the floor.

'Shut up, Thug,' Jimmy said sharply. 'We don't want any of the stray cats to hear us. Now, where's the chest?'

'Over here, Boss,' Slasher said.

Atticus watched the three magpies flutter over and perch on the edge of the shelf.

Thug nearly fell off. 'I keep losing me balance,' he wept. 'I can barely fly.'

'Don't worry, mate,' Slasher said. 'With all that lost treasure we're gonna find, you can get a tail extension.'

So they did know about the treasure. The magpies must have been eavesdropping in Nellie's garden, Atticus guessed.

'Aren't you going to arrest them?' Thomas whispered.

Atticus frowned. Now Thomas was telling *him* what to do instead of the other way around! 'I will in a minute,' he replied stiffly. He spied a ladder propped up against the wall beside the shelves. 'Wait here.' He tiptoed towards the ladder. Luckily the magpies were too engrossed in their task to notice him.

'Open the lid,' Jimmy said.

Thug and Slasher heaved open the lid of the wooden chest with their wings.

Atticus put his paw on the bottom rung of the ladder and began to climb.

The three magpies peered into the chest. 'Where's the book?' Jimmy demanded.

'It must be under them masks,' said Thug.

'Climb in there and get it out, then,' Jimmy told him.

Thug hung back. 'I don't want to,' he whimpered. 'It's scary.'

'Too bad.' Jimmy grabbed him by what was left of his tail and tipped him in.

'Chaka-chaka-chaka-chaka-chaka!' Thug's cries of protest went unheeded.

Atticus stepped off the ladder on to the top of

the three shelves. He was relieved to see that it was less cluttered than the other two. He didn't want to alert the magpies to his presence by knocking something over. One paw at a time, he crept stealthily along the shelf until he was directly above the magpies. The shelves were full of splits and knots. Atticus put his eye to one of the holes. The empty eyes of the bird mask stared back at him. Thug was somewhere underneath it.

'I can't find it,' said Thug in a muffled voice.

'Go and help him,' Jimmy told Slasher.

Slasher jumped into the chest. The two birds poked about under the masks.

'It's not here, Boss,' Slasher said.

'What do you mean, it's not there?' Jimmy's voice was menacing. 'You told me you'd seen it!'

'We did!' Slasher said. 'Honest! Someone must have taken it out.'

Jimmy leant over the chest to get a better look.

Atticus tensed. *Now was his chance.* Digging the claws of his back paws into the rough wood of the shelf to anchor himself, he swung the top half of his body over the edge and gave Jimmy a strong shove.

Jimmy was taken unawares. He toppled into the chest.

'CHAKA-CHAKA-CHAKA-CHAKA-CHAKA!'

'Surprise!' said Atticus.

The three magpies just had time to glimpse Atticus's upside-down face grinning at them before the lid banged closed, trapping them inside.

Atticus locked the chest with the kirby grip so they couldn't escape. The magpies could breathe through the keyhole. They would be all right for a little while – until he raised the alarm, anyway.

Atticus padded back towards the ladder feeling pleased with himself. He hoped Thomas was impressed! Suddenly the shed door flew open.

'Quick, Antonia, turn on the torch!' a gruff voice said.

The Tofflys! Atticus had forgotten all about them! He crouched as low as he could on the shelf. A beam of light swept round the shed, narrowly missing Atticus. Instead it fell upon Howard Toffly's wooden chest.

'There it is,' Lord Toffly said. 'You hold the torch, Antonia, I'll get it.' His progress across the shed was accompanied by a great deal of crashing and swearing.

'Be quiet, Roderick!' Lady Toffly snapped. 'Someone will hear you!' The torch beam wobbled about.

'Keep it still, Antonia!' Lord Toffly hissed. He took the chest down from the shelf, grunting and puffing with the effort.

Atticus could feel Lord Toffly's breath on his tail. It was all he could do not to twitch it.

'Get the journal,' ordered Lady Toffly. 'We don't need the chest.'

'It's locked.' Lord Toffly rattled the lid.

'Use a spoon, then!' Lady Toffly withdrew one from her pocket and threw it at her husband. It was a poor throw. The spoon clattered on to the floor. 'Darn it, just take the lot!' Lady Toffly told him. 'And hurry up! You've woken the stray cats!'

A cat-cophony of meowing was coming from the direction of Nellie Smellie's house.

Lord Toffly crashed towards the door. Lady Toffly turned off the torch.

Atticus heard the shed door bang shut and the sound of a moped revving up and puttering away down the road, pursued by a large number of yowling cats. He made his way down the ladder to where Thomas was waiting.

'Wow!' said the kitten. 'That was really, really, really cool! I want to be a police cat when I grow up, just like you!'

6

Back at the caravan park the Tofflys examined their haul. It consisted, as we know, of two hideous masks, one carved wooden chest and three magpies, none of which they particularly wanted. The one thing they did want wasn't there.

'More curses!' Lady Toffly exclaimed. 'The journal's missing. Where the heck could it have gone?'

'Nellie Smellie and her pals must have taken it out,' said Lord Toffly. He put the kettle on and threw a teabag into a mug. 'The double-crossing dirt-bags.'

'Chaka-chaka-chaka-chaka-chaka!' chattered the magpies.

'Be quiet!' Lady Toffly fastened each of their

beaks with a clothes peg and threw them into the laundry basket. 'Don't think I haven't worked out that you ruffians were after it too,' she said threateningly. She put the lid on the basket so the magpies couldn't escape and turned to her husband. 'So now what?' she said.

'We'll have to wait until Smellie and her gang take the book to the British Museum,' Lord Toffly said. He poured some milk into his tea and stirred in two crusty spoons of sugar from the packet. 'We'll steal it from there.'

Lady Toffly watched her husband with distaste. 'That place is like a fortress,' she complained. 'We'll never get past the security guards.'

'Have you got a better idea?' Lord Toffly took a noisy slurp of tea.

'Roderick, get a grip on yourself!' Lady Toffly swiped the mug from his grasp. 'Since when do we Tofflys use mugs? Where's the bone-china tea set?'

'We had to sell it to pay for the spoon cleaner,' Lord Toffly said.

Lady Toffly pulled a horrible face. 'It's too bad I didn't manage to skin that wretched police cat,' she said. 'This is all his fault.'

'I say, Antonia, you don't suppose *he* took the journal, do you?' Lord Toffly said.

The awful reality of what had happened dawned on Lady Toffly for the first time. 'Of course he did!' she wailed. 'I knew he was on to us at the car boot sale. This is his twisted idea of revenge.'

Lord Toffly gasped. 'What if he finds the spoon in the shed? He won't arrest us, will he?'

'Let him try,' Lady Toffly said recklessly. All of a sudden she burst into tears. 'I hate living in a caravan, Roderick!' she wept. 'I hate it! I hate it! I hate it! We're part of the aristocracy, for goodness' sake. We should be living at Toffly Hall and driving a Rolls-Royce, not going to car boot sales and sharing a moped. I shall go mad if I have to polish another spoon.' She flung a tin of spoon cleaner at the laundry basket.

 'How about we try to sell these?' Lord Toffly said, fingering the masks. 'Tide us over until we can have another crack at stealing the journal? You never know, Antonia, they might be worth something.'

'Well . . .' Lady Toffly sniffed. 'I suppose we could.'

Lord Toffly crossed his fingers behind his back and took a deep breath. 'Why don't we ask Benjamin if *he* can help?' he said in a wheedling tone.

Lady Toffly's eyes narrowed. Her lips pressed into a thin line. She seemed to be going through some deep inner struggle. 'Oh, very well,' she agreed eventually. 'Get Ribena on the computer.'

Ribena was Lord and Lady Toffly's grown-up daughter. She was married to an ambassador and lived abroad. And by an extraordinary coincidence the Ambassador to whom she was married was none other than Benjamin Posh-Scoundrel, the British Ambassador to Nicaragua (or Knicker-agua, as Thug called it).

Lady Toffly turned on the computer and tapped a few keys.

'Hello!' a distant voice brayed. It was Ribena.

'You talk to her, Roderick,' Lady Toffly hissed. 'You know how I feel about her marrying Benjamin!'

Lord Toffly ground his teeth. As far as he was concerned, most normal parents (by which he meant him) would think that Benjamin Posh-Scoundrel was a good match for their daughter, especially if they were as ugly as Ribena. Benjamin Posh-Scoundrel wasn't just the British Ambassador to Nicaragua; he had a first-class degree in Ancient History; spoke four hundred languages (including three hundred which were extinct); and had won an Olympic gold medal for rowing. He was also a jolly good shot, like Lord Toffly. But it still wasn't enough for Lady Toffly. She had never got over the fact that Ribena hadn't married a lord.

'Daddy, is that you?' the voice bellowed.

'Ribena!' her father shouted. 'How's Nicaragua?'

Ribena's face came into focus. She looked like a cross between a hippopotamus and a warthog, except she didn't have tusks.

'Hot,' Ribena complained.

'Is Benjamin around?'

'He's here somewhere,' Ribena said. 'He's got some frightful new parrot he's trying to train. How are things with you?'

'Could be better, Ribena old bean,' Lord Toffly admitted. 'We're a bit short of *cash*.'

'No luck on getting Toffly Hall back from those awful Tuckers, then?' Ribena asked.

'Not yet,' said Lord Toffly, 'but we did . . . er . . . come across these beauties.' He held up the masks. 'Howard brought them back from one of his expeditions.'

'What, Great-Great-Great-Uncle Howard, the famous explorer?'

'Yes. We thought Benjamin might know if they are worth something.'

'Hang on a minute. I'll get him. BENJAMIN!' Ribena shouted. 'BENJAMIN! Ah, there you are. Daddy wants to talk to you.' There was a deal of scuffling and a loud squawk as Ribena made space for her husband in front of the computer. 'Do you have to bring that detestable parrot with you everywhere?' she complained. 'Its droppings are like superglue.'

Benjamin Posh-Scoundrel appeared on the

screen. He was a very large man with a very big head and very wide shoulders upon one of which sat an enormous green parrot.

'Gosh!' said Lord Toffly. 'What happened to that bird?'

'It was flattened by a large pig.' Benjamin Posh-Scoundrel also had a very loud voice. 'The vet at Her Majesty's Prison for Bad Birds managed to reinflate it with a bicycle pump. That's why it looks like a balloon. Rather clever, don't you think?'

'Remarkable,' Lord Toffly agreed. 'What's it doing with you?'

'It's staying here until it's ready to be released back into the wild,' Benjamin said.

'Ha, ha!' said Lord Toffly. 'Then you can shoot it.'

'Shut your gob,' said the parrot.

'Well said, Pam!' It was Benjamin Posh-Scoundrel's turn to roar with laughter. 'Now, what can I do for you, Roderick?'

'We want to know how much these are worth.' Lord Toffly showed him the masks.

Benjamin Posh-Scoundrel's jaw dropped.

'Where did you get them from?' he demanded.

'A car boot sale,' Lord Toffly lied. 'They were in this.' He held up the wooden chest for his son-in-law to view.

'They belonged to Great-Great-Great-Uncle Howard, Benjamin,' Ribena's voice cut in from somewhere behind Pam. 'He brought them back from one of his expeditions.'

Benjamin Posh-Scoundrel whistled. 'Was there anything else in the chest?' he asked.

'Funny you should ask, old chap,' Lord Toffly said. 'There was a journal of Howard's; it was about some lost treasure. Something to do with jaguars.'

'Not the lost treasure of the jaguar gods?' Benjamin Posh-Scoundrel exclaimed.

'That's it!' said Lord Toffly. 'Why, have you heard of it?'

'Heard of it?' his son-in-law echoed. 'Of course I've heard of it, Roderick. It's one of the world's greatest undiscovered archaeological treasures. Where's that journal now?'

'That's the trouble,' Lord Toffly replied. 'Someone took it. We think it might be

58

the work of a local police cat known as Atticus Claw . . .'

Pam let out a loud squawk. 'CAT! CAT! CAT! CAT! CAT!' she shrieked.

'Shhhh!' Benjamin Posh-Scoundrel shut her up with a large slice of mango. 'Go on, Roderick,' he said.

'Claw and his do-gooding friends are planning to take the journal to Professor Verry-Clever at the British Museum. I thought we might have a go at – er – getting hold of it, only the security's pretty tight there, you know,' Lord Toffly said.

'You mean steal it from the museum?' Benjamin Posh-Scoundrel sounded affronted at the idea.

'Well . . . er . . .'

'It's not actually *stealing*, Benjamin.' Lady Toffly stuck her face up to the computer. 'If it belonged to Howard Toffly, then technically it's ours! Of course you'd know that if you were a lord,' she added snootily.

It was Benjamin Posh-Scoundrel's turn to grind his teeth. Some very un-ambassador-like thoughts flitted through his head. *Condescending old bat* was one of them; *stuck-up snob* was another; *big-headed battle-axe* was a third (I'm afraid the rest were too rude to print). He couldn't help not being a lord! If he were one, he'd show that silly moo a thing or two. He considered for a moment. A fantastic idea occurred to him. Maybe, if *he* could be the one to find the lost treasure of the jaguar gods and claim all the credit, Her Majesty the Queen might actually *make him into* a lord! That would shut Lady Toffly up!

'Leave it to me,' he said imperiously. 'I know exactly what to do.' His brilliant mind was already at work on a plan. 'Just get over here to Nicaragua as quickly as you can. I'll send the diplomatic bag for you first thing in the morning. And bring everything that was in that chest. *Everything*, do you hear?'

The picture on the computer screen began to flicker.

'Very well, Benjamin,' Lord Toffly said. 'But are you sure you want the magpies?'

It was too late. The connection had cut out.

'Better bring them,' Lady Toffly said. 'Just in case.'

The next day by the beach huts Atticus told Mimi about the events of the weekend.

'The Tofflys *and* the magpies!' she said. 'What a horrible combination.'

'They weren't exactly working together,' Atticus said, 'but I know what you mean.'

'What do you think the Tofflys will do with them?'

'Let them go, I suppose,' Atticus replied. 'Although I'm surprised they haven't already. I checked the magpies' nest under the pier on the way here and it's still empty.'

'Maybe Jimmy and the gang are lying low for a while,' Mimi suggested, 'in case you arrest them again.'

'Maybe,' Atticus agreed. 'They certainly left some incriminating evidence at the scene of the crime. Well, Thug did, anyway. There were quite a lot of his tail feathers on the ground. Even Inspector Cheddar managed to work out the magpies had been there.'

'What about the Tofflys?' asked Mimi. 'They're the ones who actually stole the chest. Isn't Inspector Cheddar going to arrest *them*?'

'I hope so,' Atticus sighed. 'The problem is he doesn't remember talking to anyone at the car boot sale and no one else saw them, so he's just going on the spoon that he found in the shed this morning. He's sent it off to forensics for fingerprinting.'

'That's a start,' Mimi said cheerfully, adding, 'You know him, he'll get there in the end!'

That is probably true, Atticus thought, although it might be a lot easier for everyone if Inspector Cheddar just got there in the beginning, like he did. He didn't say it though in case Mimi thought he was being mean.

'We're taking the journal to Professor Verry-Clever today,' Atticus said instead. 'Mrs Tucker is giving us a lift to the British Museum on her motorbike.'

'Is Nellie going too? And Thomas?'

'I don't think so.' Atticus hesitated. He desperately wanted to talk to Mimi about Nellie, but he didn't want to come right out and tell Mimi he suspected Nellie might be a witch, just in case Mimi thought he was being silly. He decided to tackle the subject in a more roundabout way. He fiddled with his neckerchief, wondering how to begin. 'Talking of Nellie,' he said eventually. 'She was acting very strangely yesterday.'

'What do you mean, *strangely*?' asked Mimi.

Atticus told her. 'What was really odd was that I had a bad feeling too when we got the chest down from the attic. But it passed quite quickly. I didn't pick up half the stuff she did from it.'

'She must have a sixth sense,' Mimi said slowly.

'I didn't know humans *could* have a sixth sense,' Atticus responded. 'I thought it was just animals.'

'Aisha says they can,' Mimi said. Aisha was Mimi's owner. She had a flower shop in Littleton-on-Sea and a lovely baby. 'It's just that most of them have lost it.'

'Oh,' said Atticus. Aisha was pretty switched on as far as people and animals were concerned. If that was what Aisha said, it was probably right. He decided to stop beating about the bush and ask Mimi straight out about Nellie. 'Er, Mimi, I hope this doesn't sound weird, but you don't think Nellie could be a witch, do you?'

'Maybe,' said Mimi, after a pause. 'Why? Do you?'

Atticus felt relieved. Mimi didn't seem to think the idea was ridiculous at all. He thought carefully before he answered. 'I'm not sure. I mean I don't really believe in magic but I did notice yesterday that everything about her is kind of *witchy*: the way she looks; the way she acts; all that stuff about the masks. Oh, and her Old Hag's Cure-All Ointment . . .'

'Her what?'

'It's some medicine she offered to Inspector Cheddar when he broke his tooth,' Atticus explained. 'She's even got a broomstick in the shed!' he added.

Mimi thought for a minute. 'It sort of makes sense if she *is* a witch,' she remarked after a while. 'I mean, that's probably why she's so keen on taking in cats, if you think about it. She'll be looking for her familiar.'

'What's that?'

'A cat companion,' Mimi answered. 'Not just any cat, but a special one that understands her; one that knows what *she's* thinking and she knows what *it's* thinking. That way her magic will be stronger.'

'Oh,' said Atticus. He was feeling a bit out of his depth. He didn't know anything about witches and their cats. He wasn't sure he wanted to. In fact, he rather wished he hadn't brought it up. That remark of Nellie's about her not being the only one who thought they shouldn't mess with the masks: had she actually made it or not? He still couldn't decide. And now Mimi was looking at him hard with her intelligent golden eyes as if she was mulling something important over.

'What is it?' he asked her. 'Why are you looking at me like that?'

'Well, if Nellie really is a witch and

you're the one that knows about it, then logically that can only mean one thing,' she said.

'What?' Atticus said a little sulkily. He wasn't very good at logic.

'It's obvious, isn't it?' Mimi said. '*You* must be her familiar.'

'No way!' Atticus shook his head in disbelief. He didn't like the turn the conversation had taken. The idea that Nellie could read his thoughts and vice versa was downright scary! 'I can't be! *I'm* not a witch's cat!'

'Aren't you?' Mimi said. 'Everyone apart from Inspector Cheddar knows you're special, Atticus. I wouldn't be in the least surprised if you were.'

'But I can't do magic,' he protested.

Mimi gave a delighted laugh. 'Are you sure about that? You can do everything else! Now go and find out about that lost treasure. I'm dying to know more about it.'

A little while later, at the British Museum, Mrs Tucker stepped off her motorbike and removed her leather jacket. She was wearing a different tank top today, Atticus saw, as he clambered out of the sidecar with the kids. This one said "Watch out, Edna's about!" *Nellie must have knitted her a whole drawer full*, he thought.

Professor Verry-Clever was waiting for them at the entrance. He was a tall thin man with long bony fingers and a big dome-shaped head. A pair of gold-rimmed spectacles perched on his nose. Atticus didn't remember those from the last time he had seen the Professor. He thought they made him look brainier than ever.

The Professor greeted them all warmly. 'This

way.' He led them across a huge hall full of imposing stone statues. Atticus felt slightly overawed. The statues were from ancient times. They sent a shiver down his spine. He had already learnt from experience that you had to treat the past with respect if you didn't want it to come back and bite you on the tail.

Professor Verry-Clever opened the door to his office and offered everyone a seat. He took up a position on the other side of the mahogany desk. Beside the desk was a large globe on a stand. Except it didn't show modern countries. It was a globe of the ancient world.

Mrs Tucker removed the journal from the lining of her crash helmet and handed it to the Professor.

'Goodness me!' the Professor exclaimed. 'Where did you find this?'

'It was in a chest in Nellie's attic . . .' Mrs Tucker explained everything to Professor Verry-Clever, ending with the break-in to Nellie's shed. 'Fortunately, Atticus and Thomas managed to save the book.'

'Is it valuable?' Michael asked the Professor.

'It could be,' said the Professor gravely. 'Archaeologists have been looking for the lost treasure of the jaguar gods for centuries. This appears to be an account of Howard Toffly's attempt to find it.' He opened the journal. A few loose pages fell out. They contained strange pictures, scribbled notes, some compass directions and a hand-drawn map.

'Hieroglyphs,' the Professor muttered, looking at the pictures.

Atticus regarded them curiously. He could read some hieroglyphs – ancient Egyptian ones – but he couldn't make any sense of these. A hush fell on the room as Professor Verry-Clever examined the loose sheets of paper.

'Do you know where they're from, Professor?' asked Mrs Tucker.

'Yes.' The Professor sat back in his chair and pressed his fingertips together. 'Have you heard of the mysterious Maya?' he said after a little while.

The mysterious Maya? Atticus hadn't but the children were nodding vigorously.

'We learnt about them at school,' Callie said. 'They built cities in the jungle and had writing and books and played sport and did trade and everything.'

'They died out about a thousand years ago,' Michael chimed in. 'No one really knows why – that's why they're called mysterious.'

'Absolutely right,' Professor Verry-Clever said. 'At its height the civilisation of the ancient Mayan people spread most of the way through the jungle of Central America, from what we now know as Mexico into Guatemala, Honduras and El Salvador.

Perhaps even as far as Nicaragua.' Professor Verry-Clever showed them on the globe.

'Then their civilisation died out – *boom* – just like that. No one knows why.' Professor Verry-Clever paused. 'What we *do* know is that the ancient Maya were a deeply religious people. They believed in many different gods. They also believed that the way to keep them happy was to make them offerings.'

'What sort of offerings?' Michael asked.

'Gifts, for one,' said the Professor. 'Treasure, food, that sort of thing. And, of course, sacrifices.'

'*Human* sacrifices, you mean?' asked Callie.

'Very often, yes.' The Professor nodded.

Atticus listened solemnly. Some cats he knew took offerings to their owners – like birds and mice and frogs – because they thought they would be pleased. He didn't bother, partly because he wasn't very keen on killing and partly because *his* owners didn't seem to appreciate it. The last time he'd put a dead frog in Inspector Cheddar's shoe, the Inspector had made him eat dried cat food for a week. Atticus had no idea that humans had once done the same thing. AND with their own species! It was horrible.

'Wasn't it the priests who did the sacrifices?' Michael was saying.

'Yes,' replied Professor Verry-Clever. 'The priests were very powerful. They decided who would be sacrificed and they conducted the ceremonies.' A frown creased his bulging forehead. 'Come to think of it they wore masks, like the ones Mrs Tucker has just described.'

Crumbs! thought Atticus. *That's exactly what Nellie had said.* 'The priests wore them when they made sacrifices to the gods.' He cleaned his whiskers distractedly. Nellie *had* to be a witch. It was the only possible explanation. *But where did that leave him?*

Michael was still asking questions. 'Didn't the Maya play a ball game?' he wanted to know. 'A bit like football?'

'More like volleyball,' the Professor said, 'only you couldn't use your hands. The consequences of losing were deadly. The winners

72

were treated as heroes. The losers were put to death.'

Yikes, thought Atticus. He was rubbish at ball games. He wouldn't like to have to play if one of his nine lives depended on it.

'So what exactly *is* the lost treasure of the jaguar gods, Professor?' asked Mrs Tucker.

'I'm coming to that,' the Professor replied. 'You see, the jaguar gods were the most powerful of all the Mayan gods. The Maya believed they controlled everything from the underworld to the harvest. When their civilisation collapsed, they thought it was because the jaguar gods were angry with them. So the king of the Mayan people set off on a journey from the great city of Pikan into the deepest jungle with his priests and trusted followers. The purpose of their journey was to find the valley where they believed the jaguar gods lived and persuade them to save their civilisation from destruction.'

Atticus was transfixed. It sounded epic, like some of the adventure films that Callie and Michael watched on TV.

'They took with them all the treasure they could

muster. They also took slaves to carry it. That way they had plenty to offer the jaguar gods if they found them.'

Poor slaves! thought Atticus. It was bad enough being a sacrifice but having to carry the treasure as well was taking it a bit far.

'No one knows what became of them. And no one has ever found a clue to where the valley is or where the treasure is buried.'

'Do you think Howard Toffly might have discovered something?' Callie asked excitedly.

'Quite possibly,' Professor Verry-Clever replied, squinting at the hieroglyphs.

'Then why didn't he tell anyone?' asked Michael.

'*That* is a very good question,' said the Professor. 'Perhaps this will provide the answer.' And with that, Professor Verry-Clever picked up the journal and began to read Howard Toffly's account.

In Search of the Lost Treasure of the Jaguar Gods

By Howard Toffly
1897

<u>Pikan</u>

My story begins in the ruins of Pikan, in the thick of the Honduran jungle. I had read in the newspaper that archaeologists had discovered a hieroglyph staircase there, which they believed might give a clue to the whereabouts of the valley of the jaguar gods. As a young explorer, it was my greatest ambition to find the lost treasure of the ancient Maya so I set forth at once to see the staircase for myself and offer my help on the dig. If there was a clue, I wanted to be amongst the first to see it.

Pikan proved to be a strange, mournful place. It was hard to imagine that it had once been a bustling city; for apart from the cries of birds and the chattering of monkeys it was silent as a tomb. At its centre was the Acropolis, where the royal palace had stood. Above the Acropolis a great stepped pyramid rose high into the sky. On top of the pyramid perched the altar, where the priests had performed sacrifices to the gods.

It made my blood run cold to think of it.

The hieroglyph staircase ran up one side of the Acropolis. The man in charge of deciphering it was Bruce Butterworth, an expert in ancient writing. The problem for Butterworth was that parts of the staircase had collapsed over the centuries: it was difficult to know what order the stones went in. Work on the site progressed slowly. Weeks passed into months. I began to think that Butterworth's work was doomed to failure.

Then one day out of the blue Butterworth told me he had made a discovery. He said he had found the clue he was looking for, but to my frustration he refused to tell me more. Living amongst the ruins of Pikan had made Butterworth superstitious: he believed that the jaguar gods were watching us and that they would be angry if we revealed the secrets of the ancient Maya.

Of course I pleaded with him to tell me what he knew, but Butterworth's lips were sealed. As only he could read the hieroglyphs, it seemed that the lost treasure of the jaguar gods would remain lost forever.

The Death of Butterworth

Our camp was on the edge of the jungle in a clearing beside a stream. One morning at first light I heard the sound of a tent flap opening and the soft squeak of boots. I peeped out. It was Butterworth. In his hands were a hammer and chisel.

I dressed hastily and crept after him.

Butterworth headed towards the Acropolis, to the base of the hieroglyph staircase. He searched amongst the piles of fallen stones until he found what he was looking for. Then he placed the chisel against the stone and raised the hammer. I realised with horror that Butterworth's superstitions had got the better of him: he intended to destroy the evidence that could lead us to the lost treasure of the jaguar gods so that the ancient Maya's secrets would be safe forever.

I had to stop him!

I was about to cry out when a great roar shook the air. At first I thought it was thunder but when I looked up I saw an enormous spotted cat. It was crouching on the altar at the highest point of the Acropolis.

What I had heard was not thunder but the roar of a jaguar.

Butterworth flung down the hammer and chisel and began to run. But the jaguar was too quick for him. It leapt from the altar and charged down the hieroglyph staircase after him. It fell upon Butterworth and snapped his neck before he even had time to scream. Then it pulled him off into the jungle and disappeared.

I felt numb with shock. But at the same time I saw that this was my opportunity. Only Butterworth and I knew which hieroglyphs showed the way to the valley of the jaguar gods. Perhaps, if I acted quickly, there was a way I could profit from his death. With shaking hands I took a notebook and pencil from my pocket and copied the hieroglyphs down.

Then I picked up the hammer and chisel.

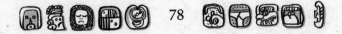

Yes, reader, I finished the work that Butterworth had started: I destroyed the hieroglyphs. But whereas Butterworth had acted from fear, I acted from greed and ambition. This was my chance to become one of the world's most famous explorers.

If I didn't find the lost treasure of the jaguar gods, then no one else would.

I ran back to the camp. Butterworth kept his notes in a carved wooden chest beneath his bed. I tore out the pages that I needed, threw them into the chest with my drawings, and left the rest of Butterworth's work beside his bed for the other members of the team to find.

Only then did I raise the alarm.

The Voyage of The Pink Dolphin

With the help of Butterworth's notes, it didn't take me long to work out what I wanted to know. According to the hieroglyphs, the valley of the jaguar gods lay approximately four hundred miles south-east of Pikan, deep in the unexplored jungle of Nicaragua. The train would take me three quarters of the way there.

The last hundred miles could only be navigated by boat.

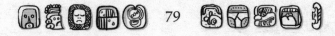

Eventually the day came when I was ready for the final leg of my journey. I had purchased a small paddle steamer, The Pink Dolphin, *which I named after the pale pink dolphins that inhabit the rivers there.*

I set my compass to the correct bearings and set off downriver.

I will never forget that first morning. I felt as if I were an ancient Mayan journeying into the complete unknown. The jungle stretched before me as far as the eye could see. I could make out the peaks of distant volcanoes and the blue veins of rivers. The vegetation was thicker than anything I had come across before. It would have been impassable on foot. I had never seen such trees – they stretched into the air like giants reaching for the sun. High above me birds whooped and sang. Enormous butterflies fluttered from flower to flower. A troop of woolly monkeys swung happily through the branches after The Pink Dolphin.

I felt on top of the world.

So it was until dark. Then the jungle became a different place. The monkeys fell silent. So did the birds. Instead the air was alive with the sound of insects and the beat of bat wings. Somewhere in the distance, I heard a jaguar roar. I moored The Pink

Dolphin *as close as I dared to the bank without her running aground, ate a frugal supper and went to bed.*

It was then that the river creatures began their attack.

What can I tell you, reader, of the horrors of that first night? Of the enormous crocodiles, the giant anaconda and the swarm of flying piranha fish that besieged The Pink Dolphin? *Of the legion of sticky leeches that crawled up my trouser legs, the army of poisonous frogs that invaded my pants, and the infestation of mini tarantula-bats that nested in my beard?*

No, reader, I cannot tell you, for if I did you would never sleep soundly in your beds again.

Somehow the journey passed. During the daytime I kept my spirits up by singing to the woolly monkeys and drinking cups of strong tea, but each night brought new terrors. Yet in spite of everything, I was excited. According to my calculations I was nearing my destination.

The valley of the jaguar gods was tantalisingly close.

On the fifth morning the river began to broaden out. At first I succeeded in keeping *The Pink Dolphin* close to the bank, where the current was weaker. But soon I lost control. The little boat was at the mercy of the river. Faster and faster we went, through the rocks and rapids. In the distance I could hear a thunderous boom. It didn't take me long to work out that it was the sound of thousands of tons of water crashing over a cliff.

We were approaching a waterfall!

There was nothing I could do except pray. *The Pink Dolphin* bobbed towards its doom. I could see the edge of the waterfall but nothing beyond that through the spray. I closed my eyes and jumped clear of the little boat. I thought I should surely drown as I tumbled through the churning water and plunged into the lake below. But then I saw sunlight above me. Somehow I managed to swim to the surface.

I had survived!

The Valley of the Jaguar Gods

I found myself in a great lagoon surrounded on all sides by lush rainforest. The lagoon was in a deep gorge that stretched for miles and miles in each direction – beyond the horizon. Ahead of me two volcanoes rose up into the clouds. Behind me the waterfall crashed and churned. I felt sure that this secret place must be where the ancient Maya had travelled a thousand years before me.

I had reached the valley of the jaguar gods.

I struck out for the shore. Butterworth's wooden chest lay in the shallows, but there was little left of the brave Pink Dolphin. *Hastily I constructed a raft from the debris, lashing it together with vines. With my penknife I fashioned a paddle from a piece of tree bark.*

As soon as I found the lost treasure, I would be ready to make my getaway.

It was then that I saw the skeleton. It sat propped up against a tree. Beside it were two masks: one the face of a bird, the other the face of a jaguar. I picked up the masks to examine them. They were the sacrificial masks of the ancient Maya, that much I knew. But what were they doing here?

My mind was racing. Had the jaguar gods left them with the skeleton as a warning for others who dared to enter their secret land? Was it true what Butterworth had said: that anyone who tried to reveal the secrets of the gods was doomed? No, I told myself. There must be some other explanation. There was no such thing as jaguar gods.

Or was there?

I glanced up. An enormous jaguar was sitting on a rock at the base of the waterfall at the mouth of a cave. From behind it, within the cave, I could see piles of precious stones sparkling against the torrents of water. My heart skipped a beat. The lost treasure! The jaguar was guarding it!

As I watched, a second jaguar emerged from the cave, then a third and a fourth. Very soon the jaguars were seven in number, sitting in a line across the face of the waterfall. They opened their great jaws and roared together. The noise was shattering, as if the earth itself were breaking.

Gods or not, I was in no doubt that these jaguars were warning me off their treasure and away from their valley.

The memory of what had happened to Butterworth came flooding back. Terrified, I threw the masks into the chest with the notes, pushed the raft out into the lagoon, jumped aboard and paddled away from the waterfall as fast as I could. Then I drifted downstream. I remember little after that. Days blurred into nights. Nights blurred into dawn. I was weak with hunger and parched with thirst. But the river creatures did not trouble me. It was as if they no longer had any interest in me now that I had been cast out of the valley of the jaguar gods.

Eventually I fell into unconsciousness. The next thing I remember was waking up on a mat of straw surrounded by villagers. Somehow my raft had found its way to the mouth of the river. A fisherman had found it floating in the sea.

I do not know how it got there, nor for how long I was unconscious.

What I do know is that the valley of the jaguar gods exists. And that one day I shall return and claim the lost treasure.

'What a cheat!' Callie said crossly.

'To think Howard Toffly kept the chest hidden in Nellie's attic so that no one else could find the lost treasure!' Mrs Tucker said hotly. 'That's exactly the sort of thing you'd expect from a Toffly!'

Back at number 2 Blossom Crescent everyone was having a late supper of cheese on toast around the kitchen table. Nellie and Thomas were there too; Thomas as a treat for helping Atticus rescue Howard Toffly's journal from Nellie's shed before the thieves took it. They were all discussing the developments of the afternoon (except Atticus and Thomas, who were eating yummy sachets of cat food in gravy and listening in).

'It's a pity Howard Toffly's dead,' said Inspector

Cheddar, 'or I'd arrest him immediately and take him down to the police station for questioning.' He did a few karate chops just to show that he meant it.

For once Atticus agreed with him. Howard Toffly was a crook. He'd stolen a valuable secret from the ruins at Pikan, destroyed the evidence with a hammer and chisel, and kept how to find the lost treasure of the jaguar gods all for himself. It was a rotten, mean, selfish thing to do.

'What did Professor Verry-Clever recommend?' asked the Inspector.

'He wants to mount an expedition to the jungle to find the treasure,' Michael said, 'so that we can return it to the people of Central America. He says he knows just the person to lead it.'

'Bravo!' said Inspector Cheddar. 'Who's going?'

'All of us!' Callie said.

'I'm not sure I can spare the time,' said Inspector Cheddar. 'I've still got to identify the owner of that spoon we found in Nellie's shed.'

Atticus rolled his eyes at Thomas.

'It was the Tofflys, Dad!' Michael said. 'It's obvious.'

'There's no such thing as obvious in the world of seaside potting-shed crime,' Inspector Cheddar said sternly. 'A good detective looks at all the evidence.'

Callie giggled. 'It's not a murder investigation, Dad!'

Just as well, Atticus thought. Inspector Cheddar would probably trip over the body without noticing it.

'It's a pity the burglars took the masks,' Mrs Tucker said, changing the subject. 'I would have liked to show them to Professor Verry-Clever.'

'I told you they were sacrificial,' Nellie remarked. She had finished her cheese on toast and was knitting a quick pair of bed socks.

Inspector Cheddar snorted.

'No, Dad, Nellie was bang-on about them,' Michael told him seriously. 'They actually *were* the sacrificial masks of the ancient Maya. That's what Professor Verry-Clever said.'

'And Howard Toffly,' Callie pitched in. 'He said so in his account.'

'It was clever of you to know that, Nellie,' Mrs Cheddar said, pouring the old lady a cup of tea.

'Yes, how on earth did you?' Mrs Tucker asked.

'Please tell us, Nellie,' Callie begged.

'Oh, all right,' said Nellie, 'as long as you promise not to tell anyone else.'

'We promise,' the children chorused.

Atticus tried to look as if he couldn't care less what Nellie was going to say. He didn't want her starting on all that witchy stuff again. He pretended to examine his claws.

'I've got second sight,' Nellie declared.

'What's that?' asked Michael.

'I can see things that are going to happen without actually seeing them, if you know what I mean. My mother had it, and her mother before that. The Smellie women have always had it, right back to old Esme Smellie who was burned at the stake for being a witch in the fifteenth century.'

Atticus wondered briefly if Esme Smellie had had a cat and, if she did, what had happened to it. His chewed ear drooped.

'Ha, ha, ha!' Inspector Cheddar laughed. 'Good one, Nellie!'

'Shut up, Dad!' Michael said. 'That's so cool, Nellie!'

'Not for Esme it wasn't,' Nellie said sharply. 'It was very hot. Luckily she made it rain and managed to escape.'

'Ho, ho, ho!' Inspector Cheddar held his sides with mirth.

Mrs Cheddar dug him hard in the ribs with her elbow.

Callie's forehead screwed into a frown. '*You're* not a witch, are you, Nellie?' she asked in awe.

'He, he, he!' Inspector Cheddar tittered quietly.

Now that was a good question. Atticus pricked up his ears. He wanted to hear what Nellie had to say. At the same time he yawned loudly as if the whole conversation bored him. He didn't want Nellie to start reading his thoughts again.

Nellie put down her knitting needles and fixed the children with a stern look. 'That's none of your business,' she replied stiffly. Her gaze shifted to Atticus. She gave him a big wink. Atticus went rigid with shock. Nellie could see right through him. She knew he was only pretending not to listen!

'Did you actually *see* someone being sacrificed yesterday when you put your hands on the chest?' Michael asked her.

90

'Maybe,' said Nellie.

'You did, didn't you?' Callie squealed. 'Who was it?'

Atticus sighed. He couldn't understand why children were so bloodthirsty. Thomas was too. The kitten was loving it. He jumped on to Callie's lap so he could hear the answer. Atticus lay down in his basket in what he hoped was a dignified police-cat sort of way that suggested the whole subject was beneath him.

'I don't know *exactly* who it was,' Nellie said. 'I didn't wait to find out. Although there *was* something familiar about them.' She scratched her armpit with a knitting needle.

'What did they look like?' asked Callie.

'They were the spitting image of your dad, as a matter of fact,' Nellie said, peering at Inspector Cheddar with her rheumy eyes.

Atticus lifted his head in surprise. *Inspector Cheddar?*

'Me?' Inspector Cheddar said, dumbfounded. 'Are you sure?'

'He was a dead ringer,' Nellie declared.

Atticus felt uneasy. The person Nellie had seen couldn't be Inspector Cheddar, could it? True, on

91

their adventures together so far Inspector Cheddar had been cursed by pirates, knocked out with a sleeping potion by a Russian criminal mistress of disguise, and almost pickled by a mad Italian art collector. But sacrificed by the ancient Maya? That sounded too bonkers, even for him.

'But it couldn't have been Dad, Nellie,' Michael reasoned. 'Because the ancient Maya died out over a thousand years ago. You must have seen something in the past, not the future.'

'In which case it was just a slave who looked like Dad who was being sacrificed,' Callie said.

'You're probably right,' said Nellie, getting back to her knitting. 'I must have got mixed up.'

'Look at the time!' Mrs Tucker got up from the table and pulled on her biker boots. 'I'd better get going. I promised I'd help Herman shampoo his beard-jumper tonight. I'll drop Nellie and Thomas off on my way home.' The three of them left. Mrs Cheddar took the kids upstairs to bed, while Inspector Cheddar loaded the dishwasher.

Atticus settled down again in his basket. He'd had a tiring day on top of a busy night. Even so, he couldn't seem to drop off. Every time he closed his eyes all he could see was Inspector Cheddar being dragged up the steps of a pyramid towards a stone altar by men in sacrificial masks. But Michael and Callie were right: it couldn't have been Inspector Cheddar that Nellie had seen. The ancient Maya were history; what Nellie had seen must have been in the past.

Atticus tried counting sardines instead. Very soon he was fast asleep.

1·1

Meanwhile, in Nicaragua, the magpies were having an even worse nightmare of their own.

'Of all the rotten luck,' Thug said. 'I mean, what are the chances of getting bird-napped by the Tofflys and ending up in Knicker-agua having to clean Pam's poo bucket?'

Slim as the chances undoubtedly were, that is exactly what had happened to Jimmy and his gang. The unfortunate trio had arrived in an overnight diplomatic bag at the British Embassy in Managua to find themselves confronted by a horrible group of people, and a revolting parrot they had hoped never to see again in their whole entire magpie lives, namely (in no particular order):

- A short fat man with a fake beard (Lord Toffly)
- A tall thin woman with a false nose (Lady Toffly)
- A woman who looked like a cross between a warthog and a hippopotamus (Ribena)
- A very large man with a very loud voice (Benjamin Posh-Scoundrel)
- A rotund parrot with severe flatulence (Pam)

And now they were engaged in scraping Pam's droppings off the sides of the bucket with a packet of Thumpers' Traditional Scrubbit and an old toothbrush.

'Pam's poo is even worse than I remember,' Slasher said, hopping on to the rim of the bucket for some poo-free air.

'That's because she's full of wind,' Thug said, hopping up beside him. 'It's since them doctors blew her up with the bicycle pump. She's like a whoopee cushion. Push her and all the gas blows out of her bum: tthththththththththththth –' he gave a rude impression – 'stop pushing her and

she fills up with air again, ready for the next plop.'
He puffed out his cheeks in an imitation of an
inflating Pam.

'It's the Boss I feel sorry for,' Slasher said.
'Imagine being married to that!'

'I'd rather marry a whoopee cushion,' said Thug.

The magpies were in the Ambassador's study. It
was a palatial room with a very high ceiling from
which hung an enormous chandelier. Attached to
its walls were the stuffed heads of various
unfortunate animals that Benjamin Posh-Scoundrel
had shot before the Nicaraguan government had
had a chance to protect them. On the polished
wooden floor lay their skins. Apart from the stuffed
heads, the room was dominated by the Ambassador's
desk; an imposing affair with numerous drawers
and a green baize top, like a billiard table. It was
piled high with important-looking papers. Besides
the papers there was just enough space for a large
red telephone, a blotting pad, a fountain pen, a glass
inkwell, an abacus, a rubber stamp saying "TOP
SECRET", a book of Latin poetry, a pyramid of
spherical chocolates wrapped in gold foil, and a pair
of antique pistols. There was no sign of a computer.

Benjamin Posh-Scoundrel preferred to do things the old-fashioned way.

'How's he getting on?' asked Thug. 'Has she still got him in a tail-lock?'

Opposite the desk stood an ornate chaise longue covered with cushions. It was from here that a loud noise issued.

'CHAKA-CHAKA-CHAKA-CHAKA-CHAKA!'

'SQUAWK! SQUAWK! SQUAWK! SQUAWK! SQUAWK!'

'No, she's just nagging him,' Slasher said.

'Blimey, she hasn't let up since we arrived!' Thug commented.

Once Pam had recovered from the shock of seeing Jimmy emerge from the diplomatic bag, she had let rip with a festering blast of pent-up resentment, which was still continuing hours later.

'CHAKA-CHAKA-CHAKA-CHAKA-CHAKA!'

'SQUAWK! SQUAWK! SQUAWK! SQUAWK! SQUAWK!'

'She's not still on about that mirror, is she?' Thug's ears were blocked with soapsuds.

Slasher cocked his head to one side. 'No. She's back to why he didn't visit her in prison.'

'Oh.' Thug cleaned his ears out with a claw. 'That again!'

'Nearly a year I was in there, Jim!' screamed Pam. 'And you never came to see me – not ONCE!'

'I've already told you, you dozy parrot, I was BUSY!' Jimmy shouted back. 'B-I-Z-Z-Y. BUSY! But you wouldn't know what that was, would you, you bird-brained cockatoo,' he yelled, ''cos you never get off your backside to do anything except order everyone else around!'

'Bit like you, Boss!' Thug joked.

Jimmy and Pam turned on him. 'Shut up and get back to work!' they chorused.

Just then the door opened. Benjamin Posh-Scoundrel strode in. Ribena trailed in his wake.

'Get off the sofa!' she screamed when she saw Jimmy and Pam fighting.

'Who's a hippopotamus?' Pam replied rudely.

Ribena went red in the face. 'Benjamin, what have you been teaching that revolting parrot?'

'I didn't teach it to say that!' Benjamin Posh-Scoundrel protested. 'It must have learnt it in Her

Majesty's Prison for Bad Birds. Come here, Pam.'
He withdrew a silk handkerchief from his breast
pocket and laid it on his shoulder. Then he scooped
Pam up carefully and perched her on top of it.

Pam gave Ribena a triumphant look. She dipped
her tail. Thhhthththtthththtthththth! A large parrot
dropping landed on the floor beside Ribena's left
foot. Ribena shook her fist at Pam.

'Temper, temper,' said Pam.

'I don't know why you dislike her so much,
Ribena,' the Ambassador said to his wife. 'I'm
rather fond of her. I shall be sad when we have to
release her into the wild.'

Pam nuzzled up to him and nibbled his ear.
'Who's a pretty boy, then?' she said.

'Stop sucking up to Benjamin,' Ribena shouted
at Pam. She vented her anger on Jimmy, shooing
him up to the top of the curtains. 'I don't know
what Mummy and Daddy were thinking, bringing
magpies here in the diplomatic bag,'
she moaned. 'As if a parrot isn't bad
enough.'

'I bet the magpies were after
Howard Toffly's journal,' Benjamin

DIPLOMATIC BAG

ONLY TO BE OPENED BY
REALLY IMPORTANT PEOPLE

said. 'Crafty little beggars got into the chest before your parents did. They want that lost treasure. You know how magpies are with shiny things.'

'Well, they can't have it,' said Ribena. 'Mummy and Daddy are Howard Toffly's nearest living relatives. It belongs to them.'

Benjamin guffawed. 'Nice try, Ribena,' he said. 'Slight problem: technically it belongs to the Nicaraguan government and the people of Central America, not your parents.'

'Oh, Benjamin, you're not going to go all clever on me, are you?' Ribena said with a sigh. 'Mummy and Daddy need this treasure. They're hard up.' Her face darkened. 'I blame the Tuckers. And that rotten police cat, Atticus Claw.'

Benjamin clapped her hard on the back. 'Don't worry, Ribena, I'm on your side really. I'd love to be the one to find the lost treasure of the jaguar gods. It would be the greatest archaeological discovery ever made: absolutely brilliant for my career. Her Majesty might even make me into a lord!'

What Benjamin Posh-Scoundrel didn't let on to Ribena was that he had been dreaming of little else for two days now, or that he'd been getting up early to practise his lordship acceptance speech in front of the bathroom mirror in four hundred languages (three hundred of which were extinct), or that he had no intention whatsoever of letting Lady Toffly get her hands on any of the treasure, which he would return to the Nicaraguan government in a blaze of publicity, or quite how much he was looking forward to rubbing Lady Toffly's nose in it when he was a lord and she was still living in a caravan polishing spoons. He imagined the headlines:

DARING BRITISH HERO
DISCOVERS LOST TREASURE

ARISE LORD POSH SAYS QUEEN
TO NEW FAVOURITE PEER

LADY TOFFLY LICKS
SON-IN-LAW'S BOOTS

He was also planning a book:

MY LIFE AS A LORD
by Benjamin Posh-Scoundrel

'You wouldn't *really* give the treasure away, would you, Benjamin?' Ribena asked suspiciously.

'Good heavens, no!' Benjamin Posh-Scoundrel lied. 'We'd just give a little bit to the Nicaraguan government, so they wouldn't suspect anything.'

Ribena seemed satisfied. 'The question is, Benjamin, how are we going to get hold of this journal of Great-Uncle Howard's. It seems as though that police cat has got everything covered. Mummy says he's a real pain in the *derrière*; so is his boss, Inspector Cheddar, and the whole of his cheesy family. Whatever you do, Benjamin, you've *got* to keep them out of it. We don't want them interfering.'

'Don't worry, Ribena,' Benjamin said. 'They won't. I'll make sure of it. Look at this.' Benjamin Posh-Scoundrel opened the top right-hand drawer of the desk, withdrew a plain manilla folder and stamped it TOP SECRET.

'What is it?'

'It's a dossier of everyone apart from us who knows about the lost treasure of the jaguar gods,' Benjamin replied. 'Take a look.'

Ribena glanced down it.

Tucker – Edna Boudica Churchill – childminder. Former MI6 Agent, code named Whelk.
Tucker – Herman Horatio – fisherman. Former
  pirate. Beard-jumper owner.

Cheddar – Ian Larry Barry Dumpling – Police
  Inspector. Formerly on traffic cone duty.
Cheddar – Mrs – events planner. Former girl.
Cheddar – Callie and Michael – schoolkids.
  Former babies.
Claw – Atticus Grammaticus Cattypuss –
  world's greatest cat detective. Former cat
  burglar.
Smellie – Nellie Hecate Bat – elderly owner
  of Littleton-on-Sea Home for Abandoned
  Cats. Former chambermaid.
Verry-Clever – Sophacles Homer – Professor
  of Ancient History. Former teacher of Lord
  BPS.

Ribena's face lit up. 'Professor Verry-Clever was your old teacher at university?'

'Yes, Ribena,' Benjamin Posh-Scoundrel said smugly. 'He taught me everything I know about Ancient History. And I'm the first person he's going to think of when he decides to mount an expedition to find the lost treasure of the jaguar gods. Who better than Benjamin Posh-Scoundrel, the British Ambassador to Nicaragua, to lead it, especially if he was once your top student?'

'Clever you!' Ribena gushed. A thought struck her. 'I say, Benjamin, you couldn't arrange it so that the Tuckers came, could you? I mean, that way if they met with a nasty accident in the jungle no one would know and Mummy and Daddy could get their house back.'

'Very well, Ribena, I will try.' If it gave his wife pleasure to arrange a nasty accident in the jungle for the Tuckers, thought Benjamin Posh-Scoundrel, then so be it. (Even though the Tofflys still wouldn't get their house back as they wouldn't actually have got any treasure!) He folded his arms across his chest and sat back and waited for the phone to ring.

BRRRING BRRRING! BRRRING BRRRING!

BRRRING BRRRING! BRRRING BRRRING!

He picked up the receiver.

'Hello,' said a voice. 'This is Professor Verry-Clever. Is that you, Benjamin?'

Benjamin Posh-Scoundrel raised a knowing eyebrow. 'Professor Verry-Clever?' he said. 'Yes, this is Benjamin. What a lovely *surprise*. How can I help?'

'Something important has come up,' Professor Verry-Clever said. 'I need your help. I want you to lead an expedition to the jungle . . .'

Benjamin Posh-Scoundrel listened politely for a few minutes, as if it were all news to him. 'Of course I will, Professor,' he said. 'On one condition.' He winked at Ribena. 'I get to choose who comes.'

1·2

A few days later Atticus stood on the quayside at Littleton-on-Sea with the Cheddars and Thomas: they had come to say goodbye to Mr and Mrs Tucker and Bones.

'I still don't understand why we're not going on the expedition,' Michael said crossly.

Atticus didn't really get it, either. All he knew was what he'd been told that morning at breakfast: the Tuckers were sailing to Nicaragua in Mr Tucker's boat, *The Jolly Jellyfish*, to find the lost treasure of the jaguar gods and they weren't. *It wasn't fair!*

'I'm sorry, darling, but that's how it is,' Mrs Cheddar said.

'Professor Verry-Clever said we could,' Callie argued.

Yeah! thought Atticus. He was feeling crosser and crosser. He was the one who'd found Howard Toffly's stuff in the first place. If it weren't for him there wouldn't even *be* an expedition.

'At least it will give us a chance to get to the bottom of the potting-shed crime,' Inspector Cheddar said.

Atticus's ears drooped. He'd already got to the bottom of the potting-shed crime: and he wanted to go with Mr and Mrs Tucker and Bones! So did Thomas. The kitten looked as fed up as Atticus felt. He started meowing piteously. Atticus joined in. Perhaps if they both made a fuss someone would listen to them!

'See!' said Callie. 'Atticus and Thomas want to go too.'

Atticus rubbed his body around her socks. At least the children understood him.

'Look, I know it's disappointing,' Mrs Cheddar sighed, 'but Professor Verry-Clever said his hands were tied.'

Professor Verry-Clever?

'But he said we could go!' Callie stamped her foot.

'I know, but he's not going on the expedition, either.'

'Who is, then?'

'The British Ambassador to Nicaragua – Benjamin Posh-Scoundrel: he's a former student of Professor Verry-Clever. Apparently the whole thing is very sensitive. Everything needs to be agreed with the Nicaraguan government. And they don't want too many people involved.'

'How come the Tuckers are going, then?' sulked Callie.

'Because Mrs Tucker is ex-MI6, that's why,' Inspector Cheddar said. 'She's got clearance.'

'Why don't we have clearance?'

There was an awkward silence.

'Unfortunately the Nicaraguan government got hold of Atticus's record,' Mrs Cheddar said quietly. 'They know he's a former cat burglar. They think that makes us a security risk.'

Atticus felt awful. He hadn't thought of that. *Was that the reason why none of them were allowed to go: because he had a criminal record?*

'But that was ages ago!' Callie said.

'It doesn't matter,' Inspector Cheddar replied sternly. 'Things like that stay on your file: it's one of the reasons why you shouldn't do them in the first place.'

Atticus hung his head. There was no need to go on about it! He followed the others along the jetty to where *The Jolly Jellyfish* was moored. Bones was busy preparing everything for the voyage. She gave Atticus a wave. Atticus waved back. Bones liked to have everything shipshape. He didn't want to disturb her concentration. She and the Tuckers had a long journey ahead of them.

Mr and Mrs Tucker were in the cabin, checking off supplies. Mrs Tucker had another tank top on today which said "Edna Rocks".

'There you aaare, Atticus!' Mr Tucker scooped him up. 'And Thomas!' He scooped the kitten up too. Come and have a look at me list to see if I's forgotten anything.'

Atticus read it carefully.

MR TUCKER'S
JUNGLE SURVIVAL KIT

Rope
Nets
Bucket
Worms
Giant parachute
Anaconda alarm
Crocodile basher
Leech squasher
Flying piranha smasher
Mini tarantula-bat repellent
Thumpers' Traditional Fart Spray
Beard-jumper shampoo

'What's the giant parachute for?' asked Callie.

'That's to attach to the *The Jolly Jellyfish* so we can parachute over the waterfall without getting smashed to smithereens like *The Pink Dolphin* did.'

What about the fart spray?' asked Michael.

'That's to put in me pants to get rid of the poisoned frogs.'

'Eeerrrgggh!' said Callie.

Eeerrrrggggh! was about right, thought Atticus. He didn't think there would be many frogs brave enough to jump into Mr Tucker's pants anyway.

'How about I sing a quick sea shanty to get us in the mood for the voyage?' Mr Tucker said, putting down the cats.

'We're not going on the voyage,' Michael said gloomily.

'All the moorrrre reason for a shanty, then!' Mr Tucker insisted. 'It'll lift your spirits.'

He began tapping his wooden leg on the floor.

Atticus felt his tail twitching to the beat. Mr Tucker's voice rang round *The Jolly Jellyfish*.

'I's got me alarm and I's got me basher,
I's got me worms and I's got me smasher,
Don't youze go messing with Herman Tucker,
Or you'll get it in the neck, you beastly bloodsucker!'

'What happens if you meet the jaguar gods?' asked Callie.

'There's no such thing as the jaguar gods,' Inspector Cheddar said.

Atticus sighed. He wished Inspector Cheddar would stop saying things like that. It almost certainly meant that there *was* such a thing as the jaguar gods if he said there wasn't!

'What about the jaguars that Howard Toffly saw, then?' Callie argued back.

'Yeah, Dad, he said they were protecting their territory.' Michael stuck up for his sister.

'And their treasure.' Callie stuck up for her brother.

'That was over a hundred years ago,' said the Inspector. 'They'll be well dead by now.'

Atticus just hoped the Tuckers would be all right without him. Even if the jaguars weren't gods and the ones that Howard Toffly had seen *were* dead, there might still be lots of others in the jungle.

'Professor Verry-Clever says the jaguars will be wary of humans,' Mrs Tucker said. 'He says the Ambassador will take care of them if they do attack.'

'How?' asked Michael.

'I don't know. I suppose he'll bring a tranquillizer gun. Apparently he's a very good shot.'

Atticus's eyes narrowed. He instinctively didn't like people who were very good shots. It usually meant they'd been practising on animals. He hissed.

'Don't youze worry, Atticus,' Mr Tucker said soothingly. 'I reckons it's mainly the deadly river creatures we needs to look out for, not the jaguaarrrrrs. I reckons they'll leave us well alone.'

Atticus wished he were going. If only the Ambassador hadn't found out about his cat burgling!

'Isn't it going to take an awfully long time to get to Nicaragua?' Michael said.

'Nope,' Mr Tucker said. He pointed to some red canisters stored at the rear of the boat. 'I's got a fresh supply of shaaark faaarrt. We'll be there in no time.'

Shark fart was Mr Tucker's favourite fuel. It made *The Jolly Jellyfish* go like a rocket.

'What about medicine?' asked Mrs Cheddar.

'Bones packed the first-aid kit,' Mrs Tucker told her. 'We've got most things. And Nellie gave me some of her Old Hag's Cure-All Ointment in case Herman gets his other leg bitten off by a crocodile.'

Inspector Cheddar snorted. 'Fat lot of good that will do!' he said.

Mrs Tucker ignored him. 'She made us these as well.' She pulled two big brown onesies out of a bag. 'They're woolly monkey suits apparently.'

'What do you need those for?' asked Callie.

'I have absolutely no idea!' Mrs Tucker said. 'Nellie said she thought they might come in handy.' She stuffed them back into the bag.

Atticus frowned. *Woolly monkey suits? What was Nellie up to this time?*

'Right! We'd better be going!' Mrs Tucker gave Callie and Michael a hug. 'We'll send you a postcard via the Embassy so it gets here quickly.' She turned to her husband. 'Have you got Howard Toffly's book and all the bits of paper, Herman? I told you to put them in a safe place.'

'Aye, they's in me sock drawer.'

'That doesn't sound very safe,' Callie objected.

'You obviously haven't smelt Herman's socks,' Mrs Tucker said with a shudder. 'Bye, Atticus!'

Atticus gave a dejected purr. It just didn't feel

right saying goodbye. He wanted everyone to go on the adventure.

Mrs Cheddar led the way back to the quay.

'Bye!' Everyone waved.

Mr Tucker started the engine. ZIP! *The Jolly Jellyfish* shot off. Very soon it was out of sight.

'Hang on a minute,' said Callie as they walked back to the car. 'Where's Thomas?'

'He was here a minute ago,' said Michael. 'At least, I saw him when we were on the boat.'

Mrs Cheddar put her hand to her mouth. 'He must have stowed away!'

'I expect that was your idea.' Inspector Cheddar rounded on Atticus. 'You're supposed to be setting a good example, not teaching kittens to be stowaways!' Atticus's ears drooped. It wasn't his idea but he wished it had been. Why hadn't *he* thought of stowing away? Now Thomas was going to have all the fun. He felt a pang of regret. Stowing away was the sort of thing he would have done when he was a cat burglar. He wouldn't have thought twice about it then. An awful thought struck him. Maybe being a police cat had made him, well – *boring*.

POSTCARDS FROM THE TUCKERS

(SENT VIA THE DIPLOMATIC BAG)

Dear Callie, Michael and Atticus,

We have arrived safely in Nicaragua. Benjamin Posh-Scoundrel, the Ambassador, came to meet us at the port. He is a very big man with a very loud voice and his wife (Ribena) looks like a cross between a hippopotamus and a walrus – sorry, make that a warthog. They invited us to lunch at the Embassy to plan the expedition, which was lovely (although the place did stink of bird poo for some reason). The Ambassador offered to keep Howard Toffly's journal and the map and so on in a safe place for us until we got to the jungle, but we said no in case the beastly Tofflys found out and tried to steal it again. Ribena had some sort of fit at that point and had to leave the table. Apparently she suffers from the heat, so she often has to lie down, although she is coming on the expedition, which seems a bit silly as it will be very hot in the jungle.

Lots of love,
Mrs Tucker

PS Guess who we found hiding in my tank tops? Yes, Thomas – the naughty rascal! Tell Nellie not to worry – he's fine. He's learning the ropes from Bones. Mr Tucker says he'll make a great ship's cat.

Dear Callie, Michael and Atticus,

We have been travelling upriver for the last two days and have finally reached the place where Howard Toffly began his journey on The Pink Dolphin. The jungle is incredibly thick. The only way to get through it is by boat. Howard Toffly was right: it is like travelling back in time a thousand years to when the ancient Maya came.

Talking of boats, the Ambassador and Ribena have hired their own: there isn't enough room for everyone on The Jolly Jellyfish because Benjamin is so huge. They've called it The Toffly Treasure Hunter, which is a pretty good name, although I did joke with Ribena that – unlike Howard Toffly – we will have to give all the lost treasure to the Nicaraguan government if we find it instead of keeping it for ourselves. The poor woman started foaming at the mouth and had to go and have another lie-down. I really don't think she should have come.

Lots of love,
Mrs Tucker

PS Thomas doesn't seem to like Ribena or the Ambassador. He keeps sniffing them in a very peculiar way. I'm not sure why. Maybe it's the smell of bird poo? They seem to carry it around with them.

Dear Callie, Michael and Atticus,

We are setting off into the jungle in an hour so this is the last postcard I'll be able to send until we return. It seems like it's not going to be just the four of us after all. Ribena told me this morning that she'd invited her mum and dad as well. I said I didn't think that was a very good idea but she insisted. She said her dad is a very good shot, like Benjamin, so if we meet any crocodiles he can blast them. I said I didn't think you were allowed to shoot crocodiles any more and Mr Tucker was just going to use a basher to give them a fright, whereupon Ribena had another one of her fits and had to go and lie down AGAIN. I'm really not sure she's up to this! Hopefully her parents will look after her. I haven't actually met them yet: so far they've been holed up in The Toffly Treasure Hunter.

Anyway, wish us luck! You'll be pleased to know Mr Tucker isn't taking any chances with the poisonous frogs. He's already got his fart powder out. He offered to put some in Ribena's pants, which is maybe another reason why she had a funny turn.

Lots of love,
Mrs Tucker

PS Thomas is behaving very strangely. This morning he brought me some magpie feathers. There aren't any magpies in Nicaragua so I think he must have got them from Nellie's shed. Goodness knows why he brought them on board The Jolly Jellyfish! Maybe it's some kind of offering, like the ancient Maya? It's a pity Atticus isn't here – I'm sure he'd know what it meant!

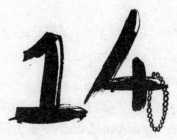

'I don't think it's an offering, I think it's a clue,' said Atticus.

It was Saturday. He and Mimi were sharing an ice cream by the beach huts while they discussed the postcards. Callie and Michael had gone for a swim with Mrs Cheddar. Inspector Cheddar was at the police station processing parking tickets. Luckily it was Atticus's day off. He had other things he wanted to do.

'What kind of a clue?' said Mimi.

'Well, the magpies aren't *here*, are they?' Atticus said meaningfully. He had checked the nest under the pier every day since their disappearance and there was still no sign of them.

'You think they're in Nicaragua?' Mimi said in surprise.

'Why not?' Atticus argued. 'They tried to steal Howard Toffly's journal. They want that lost treasure as much as anyone.'

'But how did they get to Nicaragua?' Mimi said.

'They must have gone with the Tofflys.' Atticus had been thinking about it a lot. If he couldn't actually be *on* the expedition, he was jolly well going to work out what was happening in his absence. He was still the world's greatest cat detective, even if he was stuck in Littleton-on-Sea. 'Don't forget the Tofflys have disappeared too,' he said.

'Good point,' said Mimi. She took a lick of ice cream.

'No one knows where they've gone,' Atticus continued. 'The caravan's closed up. They haven't been seen since the night of the raid on Nellie's shed.'

'Has Inspector Cheddar checked the airports?' Mimi asked, cleaning her whiskers with her paw.

'Yes,' said Atticus. 'And the ports. That's the funny thing. There's no record of them leaving the country.' He wanted to add, 'He should just have arrested them when he had the chance,' but stopped himself. There was no point in crying over spilt milk. Better to lap it up and get on with things.

'They could have gone in disguise,' Mimi suggested. 'Weren't they wearing disguises at the car boot sale?'

'Well, yes,' Atticus said, biting off a chunk of wafer, 'but they were awful. I don't think anyone except Inspector Cheddar would have fallen for them.'

'So how did they get out of the country?'

Atticus shrugged. 'I don't know. They must have found some other way.'

'And how did they find out that the lost treasure of the jaguar gods is in Nicaragua?' Mimi said.

'I don't understand that, either,' Atticus admitted. 'I've just got this hunch.' He frowned. 'I'm sure Thomas is trying to tell Mrs Tucker something. I just don't know what.'

'Mrs Tucker says Thomas doesn't like the

Ambassador and his wife,' Mimi said, looking at the second postcard again.

'It also says they smell of bird poo,' Atticus said thoughtfully.

'So?'

'Well, what if it's magpie poo they smell of?'

'You think the *Ambassador* is mixed up in this?' Mimi said in surprise.

'Maybe,' Atticus said. 'I've been thinking about it, Mimi. The Ambassador could have persuaded the Nicaraguan government to let me go on the expedition. Professor Verry-Clever didn't seem to think there would be a problem.'

'What about your criminal record?' Mimi reminded him gently.

Atticus shook his head. 'Callie was right. That was ages ago. And look at everything I've done since then. I've saved Inspector Cheddar's life loads of times. And I rescued all that priceless art. I even stopped the Crown Jewels from being stolen' – it was true: he had – 'everyone knows that. The Queen would have stuck up for me to the Nicaraguan government if the Ambassador had asked her. So would the Prime Minister. I reckon the fact I was once a cat burglar is an excuse – I mean Mr Tucker was once a pirate but no one stopped him from going. The Ambassador doesn't want me there. I just need to find out why.' He got up. 'Come on.'

'Where are we going?'

'To have a look round the Tofflys' caravan,' Atticus said. 'Maybe *they* have left a clue.'

'How will we get in?' Mimi said.

'Leave that to me,' Atticus purred.

A little later the two cats stepped off the bus beside the caravan park. 'This way.' Atticus led Mimi to a seedy-looking caravan at the edge of the park. Some of the caravans were very smart and had pots of pretty flowers outside, but this one was a wreck.

'Why is it in such a state?' Mimi asked.

'Because the Tofflys think someone else should do everything for them,' Atticus replied. 'They can't be bothered to do anything themselves.'

Mimi tried the door. 'It's locked.'

'There's a window open here,' Atticus said. 'Give me a minute.' He braced his back paws and sprang, grabbing on to the window ledge with his front claws. He hauled himself up and balanced on the ledge. Then he measured the gap with his whiskers. They just fitted. That meant the rest of him would too. He squeezed under the window and dropped down to the floor inside the caravan.

Quickly he unlocked the door for Mimi. The two cats looked around. The inside of the caravan was even more of a mess than the outside. Washing-up was piled high in the sink. Spoons littered the floor. A mug of tea, which had been left on the table, was growing a skin of mould. The Tofflys had obviously left in a hurry. There was no sign of Howard Toffly's chest.

'What exactly are we looking for?' asked Mimi.

'I'm not sure,' Atticus said. 'Anything that ties the Tofflys or the magpies to Nicaragua. And to Benjamin Posh-Scoundrel.'

'Okay.'

The two cats started searching.

'There's some magpie feathers in the laundry basket,' Mimi said. 'So Jimmy and the gang were definitely here.'

'That's a start,' Atticus said. 'Keep looking.'

The two cats searched through all the cupboards and drawers.

'It looks like the Tofflys have taken their passports,' Atticus said in frustration, when the search turned up nothing. 'So how come they haven't used them?' He jumped on to the top of a cabinet and started rifling through some boxes of spoons.

'I'm trying to think,' said Mimi. 'They must have got VIP passes or something. I'll go and check in the bedroom.'

Atticus threw the spoons back into the last box. One of them missed, knocking over a silver photograph frame that had been turned towards the wall. Atticus picked it up and glanced at the photo. He blinked. The photo was of a very large man with very wide shoulders and a very big head getting married to a woman who looked like a cross between a warthog and a hippopotamus. Next to the bride was a beaming Lord Toffly. And at the bottom of the photo frame was an inscription:

TO DARLING DADDY
FROM RIBENA

So that was the connection! 'Mimi!' he called. 'I've found something.'

Mimi raced over.

'Ribena Posh-Scoundrel is Lord and Lady Toffly's daughter!' Atticus said.

'Which makes Benjamin Posh-Scoundrel their son-in-law!' Mimi whispered. 'The Tofflys must have taken the magpies to Nicaragua.' She clapped a delicate paw to her whiskers. 'Didn't the last postcard from Mrs Tucker say that Ribena's *parents* had come along for the trip?'

Atticus gasped. 'You're right, Mimi! It all fits. That's what Thomas was trying to tell Mrs Tucker. He must have found out that the Tofflys and the magpies were hiding on board *The Toffly Treasure Hunter* and taken her the magpie feathers as evidence.'

'No wonder Benjamin Posh-Scoundrel didn't want *you* there!' Mimi said. 'I guess it's lucky that Thomas *did* stow away, otherwise you'd never have worked out the truth.' Her golden eyes gleamed. 'I think I know how the Ambassador got them all out of the country!'

'How?'

'The diplomatic bag.'

'What's that?' Atticus asked.

'It's the way governments send things backwards and forwards from their embassies in different countries without anyone else seeing them,' Mimi said. 'It's supposed to be for letters and parcels. Benjamin Posh-Scoundrel must have used it to smuggle his parents-in-law out.'

'And the magpies,' Atticus reminded her.

'What are we going to do?' Mimi said.

'We'll show Mrs Cheddar and the kids the photo,' Atticus said. 'The Tuckers could be in grave danger. My guess is the only reason they were allowed to go to Nicaragua is because the Tofflys want revenge on them for being booted out of Toffly Hall. They must be warned about Ribena and her revolting family before it's too late.'

'But you can't reach them by phone.'

'Then we'll just have to go to the jungle!'

'Do you think you'll get there in time?' Mimi

asked anxiously. It was over a week since the Tuckers had left.

'I don't know, but we have to try,' Atticus said. 'Those villains are capable of anything.' He snatched up the photo in his teeth and the two cats hurried out of the caravan and headed back to the beach.

Part One
Littleton-on-Sea
Part Two

15

Meanwhile, on board *The Toffly Treasure Hunter*, Thug was in a strop. 'I hate Knicker-agua,' he moaned. 'I want to go home.'

The magpie gang had been smuggled on to *The Toffly Treasure Hunter* under cover of darkness, with Lord and Lady Toffly, just before the two vessels – *The Toffly Treasure Hunter* and *The Jolly Jellyfish* – set off upriver on their expedition to find the lost treasure of the jaguar gods.

The interior of *The Toffly Treasure Hunter* was, in fact, luxurious. There was a large seating area with fitted sofas, a coffee table laden with bowls of fruit and trays of nibbles, and a drinks cabinet stocked with the finest champagne. Beyond the seating area a decent-sized galley kitchen full of yummy-smelling grub led through to three en-suite cabins with extra-large beds (to accommodate the Ambassador's extra-large body). *The Toffly Treasure Hunter* also boasted toughened glass, steel doors, a state-of-the-art radar system, automatic river creature defences and a gun safe stuffed with enough firearms to support a small army.

The only thing it didn't have was a parachute.

The problem for the magpies was that they weren't free to enjoy any of *The Toffly Treasure Hunter*'s considerable comforts. Instead they were confined to a small metal birdcage suspended from the ceiling by a large hook. The Tofflys, meanwhile, were taking an afternoon nap in their cabin, while the Ambassador and his wife were on deck, slowly navigating their way along the river behind *The Jolly Jellyfish*.

Thug scratched his wing-pit vigorously. 'Those mini tarantula-bats are a pain in the bum,' he announced.

Thug had had a difficult twenty-four hours. Unfortunately, despite all the Ambassador's precautions, several hundred of the tiny beasts had got in overnight after Pam the parrot had drunk too much champagne and opened the window to be sick. The mini tarantula-bats had swarmed in and started nesting in Thug's feathers. It had taken several squirts of Ribena's best perfume to get rid of them.

'I don't see why we're stuck in here while *she* gets to lord it with Benjamin Poshface,' Thug continued peevishly. He cast a dirty look in Pam's direction.

The parrot had assumed pride of place on the comfiest cushion next to the large dent in the sofa where the Ambassador habitually sat.

'Cos Poshface thinks we'll escape and steal the treasure,' Slasher explained to his mate. 'Whereas Pam's so fat she can barely get airborne.'

'Neither can I,' said Thug gloomily. 'Only not cos I'm fat,' he added hastily. 'Cos me tail's still moulting.' He scratched his bottom feverishly. A few more feathers fell out.

'You *sure* Ribena got rid of all of them mini tarantula-bats?' Slasher asked suspiciously.

'Yeah,' Thug said. 'They all snuffed it when they sniffed it – Ribena's perfume, I mean, not my bum.'

'I'm not surprised they snuffed it,' Jimmy

Magpie said sourly from his position at the far end of the perch. 'That perfume smells fruitier than one of Pam's burps.'

'Maybe you're hallergic to it?' Slasher suggested to Thug.

'Yeah, maybe,' Thug agreed. 'I've got very sensitive skin. Talking of fruit,' he said, changing the subject, 'I'm hungry.'

'Me too,' said Slasher.

The two magpies eyed Pam with envy. The parrot had just finished shovelling peanuts down her throat and was tucking into another mango. Thick, sticky, yellow juice dribbled down her beak on to her green chest feathers.

'Can't you ask her for some, Boss?' Thug begged.

'No,' Jimmy said.

'Please?' wheedled Slasher. 'I'm starving.'

'Oh, all right.' Jimmy was hungry too. He poked his beak through the bars of the cage and put on a charming voice. 'Oh, Pam, er, honey, you're looking particularly lovely today. That mango-juice stain really suits your colouring. Any chance of a bit of fruit for your loving husband and his pals?'

'Get stuffed,' Pam said.

Just then Benjamin Posh-Scoundrel and Ribena climbed down the stairs from the deck into the cabin. Ribena banged the door shut and locked it behind her. 'I'm warning you, Benjamin, I can't stand much more of those insufferable Tuckers and that disgustingly cute kitten of theirs,' she said. 'What's its name?'

'Thomas,' replied her husband, sinking into the dent on the sofa next to Pam and wiping the juice dribble off her feathers tenderly with his handkerchief. 'The ship's cat is called Bones.'

'It's the kitten who's the troublemaker,' said Ribena. 'I've a good mind to ask Daddy to shoot it, the nosy little beggar. I told you I found it trying to get into the cabin before we set off, didn't I? I've got a nasty feeling it's on to us.'

'Stop worrying about Thomas, Ribena,' said Benjamin Posh-Scoundrel. 'The important thing is that the Tuckers don't suspect a thing.'

Benjamin Posh-Scoundrel felt even more pleased with himself than he usually did. He had successfully ditched almost everyone involved in the original trip, including Professor Verry-Clever.

Now all-he had to do was find Howard Toffly's journal, lose the Tuckers, 'borrow' Mr Tucker's parachute to get over the waterfall and find the treasure (without Lady Toffly getting her mitts on it). Then he would claim all the glory for himself and wait for the 'Arise, Lord Posh' tap on the shoulder from Her Majesty the Queen.

'The sooner we arrange a nasty accident for the Tuckers and their rotten cats, the better . . .' Ribena was saying.

'I totally agree, Ribena,' Benjamin Posh-Scoundrel said, dragging himself back to the present. 'What did you have in mind?' Being nearly a lord made him feel generous-spirited towards his wife.

'Well, it's not so much what I have in mind; it's more what Mummy and Daddy want to do,' said Ribena slyly.

'And what would that be?' her husband asked.

'If you must know, they want us to raid *The Jolly Jellyfish* at dawn and chase the Tuckers into the jungle so the jaguars can eat them,' Ribena said. 'Either that or the Tuckers will be hopelessly lost forever and starve to death. Or caught up in an enormous spider's web and have their blood sucked out by a giant tarantula. Or . . .'

'Yes, yes, Ribena, I get it.' Benjamin Posh-Scoundrel raised a bushy eyebrow. 'Can't we just put a hole in *The Jolly Jellyfish* and leave them marooned for a bit until someone comes to rescue them?' he suggested mildly.

'Oh, come *on*, Benjamin,' Ribena stormed. 'Stop being such a spoilsport. I think it's perfectly reasonable for us to raid them after what the Tuckers have done to Mummy and Daddy! Besides, we need to get Great-Uncle Howard's book. The Tuckers aren't just going to hand it over, are they?'

That was true, thought the Ambassador. Without the map (which the Tuckers showed no sign of giving up) they couldn't navigate their way to the treasure. Ribena was right for once: it would be better to be shot of the Tuckers altogether. 'Very well, Ribena,' he agreed, 'a dawn raid on *The Jolly Jellyfish* it shall be. If anyone asks what happened to the Tuckers when we get back, we'll say they got eaten by the flying piranha fish.'

'Thank you, Benjamin.' Ribena grinned at him toothily.

'You are most welcome, my dear,' Benjamin Posh-Scoundrel said in his most lordly voice. He glanced out of the window. It was getting dark. 'Now, let's batten down the hatches and tell your parents to prepare for the raid.'

16

A few days after his discovery of the incriminating photo in the Tofflys' caravan, Atticus found himself in Nicaragua with the party of rescuers. The group consisted of Atticus, Mimi (whom Aisha had agreed could join them), the Cheddars, Professor Verry-Clever and Nellie Smellie (who had insisted on coming along 'just in case they needed a bit of knitting doing').

Atticus didn't think they'd need any knitting doing. It was boiling hot in the jungle. Luckily his fur acted as an insulator in both directions: when it was cold it kept him warm, and when it was hot it kept him cool. As long as he stayed in the shade, he'd be fine.

This time there had been no problem about him joining the expedition. Her Majesty the Queen had spoken personally to the Nicaraguan president. It turned out that Benjamin Posh-Scoundrel hadn't even *mentioned* the discovery of Howard Toffly's journal to their government, let alone discussed mounting an expedition to find the lost treasure of the jaguar gods. The whole 'security' issue surrounding Atticus's involvement had been a sham just to keep Atticus and the Cheddars out of things. Everyone agreed it was because Benjamin Posh-Scoundrel, Ribena and the Tofflys were planning to steal the lost treasure of the jaguar gods for themselves, except Professor Verry-Clever who thought his former student might just want to claim all the glory for himself because he'd always been a bit of a big-head.

Either way Atticus had been given clearance at the highest level. A warrant had also been issued for the arrest of the villains.

'You'll find everything on board you need.' The Commander of the Nicaraguan army had come to see them off. He spoke perfect English with a lilting Central American accent.

Atticus meowed his approval. The Nicaraguan government had supplied them with an attack-proof amphibious assault vehicle to keep out the deadly river creatures. At least he and Mimi didn't have to worry about mini tarantula-bats getting in their fur.

'What does this do?' Michael pointed to a big red lever.

'It transforms the vehicle from a boat into a tank,' the Commander said. 'When you get to the waterfall

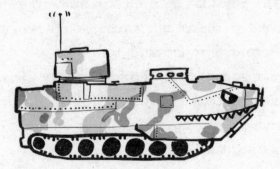

you can cut across land and find another way down to the valley without going over the fall.'

Even cooler! thought Atticus. He'd been worrying about the waterfall. He didn't like getting wet and they didn't have a parachute, like Mr Tucker did.

'How do we get out of the valley?' asked Michael.

'You'll have to carry on downstream until you get to the sea. I warn you though, that part of the jungle is still completely unchartered, even by Howard Toffly. We won't be able to pick up any signal from you until you reach the river mouth. But don't worry; you have plenty of supplies. And the vehicle is equipped with powerful headlights so you can travel at night. Good luck.' The Commander returned to his jeep and sped off.

Mrs Cheddar took the controls. 'Which way, Professor?' she asked, switching on the engine.

'According to Howard Toffly, the valley of the jaguar gods is here.' Professor Verry-Clever had brought a copy of Howard Toffly's papers with him. He spread out the photocopied map to show Mrs Cheddar.

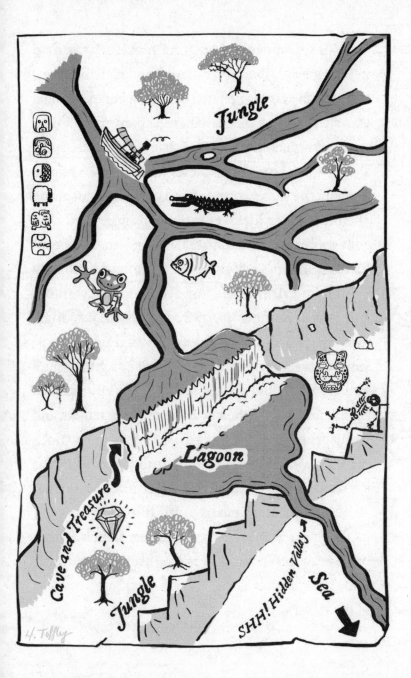

It was the first time Atticus had seen the map properly. The river had lots of tributaries, which zigzagged across the page. It also showed the places where the river creatures had attacked *The Pink Dolphin*.

Professor Verry-Clever set the co-ordinates using the ship's compass and off they went along the brown, muddy river into the jungle.

It was Atticus's turn to feel like an ancient Mayan setting off on a great journey. He had been to a rainforest once before on a different adventure, but it was nothing compared to this. The jungle was magnificent. The trees stretched up as far as he could see, their leaves spreading in a great green canopy high above them in the sky. Vines as thick as snakes twisted their way up the tree trunks and hung from branches like ropes. The forest floor was a sea of lush vegetation with leaves as big as soup plates and huge colourful flowers that thrust their petals towards the light.

But it was the noise that struck Atticus the most. It was like listening to music played by an orchestra made up entirely of animals. He could hear birds calling, monkeys chattering, insects buzzing, crickets chirping, even the beat of wings. The only thing he couldn't hear was a jaguar's roar; but the jaguars would be wary of a party of humans – at least that's what Mrs Tucker had said.

The amphibious vehicle zipped along. They were travelling much faster than Howard Toffly would have done in *The Pink Dolphin*. Atticus felt his spirits lift. Maybe they would be able to reach the Tuckers before the Tofflys struck!

Mimi was sitting on the front deck with Callie, Michael and Nellie. Atticus went to join them. The kids were making a scrapbook. They busied themselves by taking photos of the jungle and jotting down notes about the plants and animals they could see through the binoculars.

Nellie, meanwhile, was hunched over her knitting. *Clickedy-clickedy-click!*

'What's Nellie knitting this time?' Atticus asked Mimi. It looked like an enormous pair of pants.

'Some frog-proof bloomers,' Mimi said.

'Oh.' Atticus wished he hadn't asked. He eyed Nellie warily. So far since they'd arrived in Nicaragua she hadn't actually *tried* anything witchy with him, but he had the sneaking suspicion it wouldn't be long before she did. 'What's she doing here anyway?' he complained to Mimi. 'We don't need any knitting doing. It's about thirty degrees in the shade.'

'I guess we'll just have to wait and see.'

Atticus felt grumpy. It was all very well Mimi saying that, but *she* wasn't the one Nellie was trying to recruit as her familiar! He decided to adopt an attitude of lofty indifference by turning his back on Nellie and cleaning his whiskers.

Inspector Cheddar came and sat down. 'Ah,' he said, 'the jungle! Makes you think of Tarzan.' He let out a blood-curdling cry. 'Ah-a-ah-a-ah-a-ah-a-ah!'

There was a huge commotion amongst the forest animals. Callie and Michael giggled. Atticus put his hands over his ears. He looked blankly at Mimi. 'Who's Tarzan?'

'He was a character in a book,' she told him. 'He

was brought up in the jungle by apes and learnt to live like they do. He used that cry to summon the apes.'

'Oh,' said Atticus. Judging by the racket going on in the treetops, Inspector Cheddar seemed to have summoned just about *everything*, including a troop of woolly monkeys, which were swinging merrily after them through the branches, chattering raucously.

Just then they rounded a bend in the river.

'Mum! Stop!' Callie shouted.

Atticus's ears drooped. On the bank, marooned in the mud was *The Jolly Jellyfish*.

Mrs Cheddar slowed the amphibious vehicle down to a chug and directed it towards the bank. She flipped the big red switch to the TANK setting, drove it out of the water on to the mud and stopped a few metres from the stranded vessel.

'AHOY THERE!' Inspector Cheddar had brought a megaphone with him.

There was no answer from the boat. Atticus's tail twitched in concern. *The Jolly Jellyfish* had a thoroughly deserted air about it.

'COMING ABOARD!' Inspector Cheddar shouted through the megaphone. 'AH-A-AH-A-AH-A-AH-A-AH!'

Inspector Cheddar's cry was answered by an even louder commotion from the animals. The treetops shook with life. More woolly monkeys joined the crowd that had already gathered. Atticus wished Inspector Cheddar would shut up. Some of them didn't look that friendly!

The kids helped Mrs Cheddar lower the gangplank between the two vessels to make a bridge across the muddy bank. 'Stay here and look after Nellie and the Professor; just in case it's an ambush,' Atticus told Mimi.

Mimi nodded. 'Okay. Be careful.'

Atticus scampered across the gangplank after Mrs Cheddar and the kids.

'Thomas?' he meowed. 'Bones?'

It was no good. *The Jolly Jellyfish* had been abandoned. But there was still plenty of crashing going on above them. Atticus raised his head. The troop of brown woolly monkeys peered down at him from the jungle canopy. To his surprise one of them grabbed hold of a vine and flew towards him. It landed on the deck of *The Jolly Jellyfish* with a thud.

Atticus blinked. It wasn't a monkey at all. It was Mrs Tucker! She was wearing the brown woolly-monkey onesie that Nellie had knitted her! He sighed. Maybe he'd been wrong about them not needing Nellie's knitting. It had obviously come in useful for the Tuckers.

'Mrs Tucker!' the kids cried.

Mrs Tucker put her fingers in her mouth and gave a sharp whistle. 'Bones!' she called. 'Thomas!'

The two cats hurtled through the trees and landed at her feet.

Mrs Tucker threw back the hood of her onesie. 'Thank goodness you're here,' she said. 'I don't think I could have stood another day grooming Mr Tucker's beard-jumper. Now give me a hand to get him down. We'll have to use the bucket.'

'What happened?' Callie asked when Mr Tucker had been safely lowered from the trees on to the deck of *The Jolly Jellyfish*.

'We were raided,' Mrs Tucker said grimly.

'By the Tofflys?' Michael guessed.

'How did you know?' asked Mrs Tucker.

'Atticus found a photograph in the Tofflys' caravan of Ribena and Benjamin Posh-Scoundrel's wedding,' Mrs Cheddar explained. 'We worked it out from there.'

Thomas trotted over to Atticus and rolled over playfully. 'Don't you think it was clever of me to find the magpie feathers?'

'Of course it was!' Atticus purred gruffly. He was happy to see Thomas. Jungle life seemed to be suiting the kitten. He was as playful and cheeky as ever. 'You are a great detective. Like me!'

Thomas looked pleased.

'Although it was very naughty of you to stow away,' Atticus added sternly. He didn't want Thomas thinking he could get away with anything.

'That beastly parrot, Pam, is in on it too,' Mrs Tucker was saying. 'She's Benjamin Posh-Scoundrel's pet.'

Atticus's ears pricked up. *Pam!* He hadn't expected that. He didn't think Jimmy Magpie would have done, either. That must have been a nasty surprise for the magpie boss.

'But she got squashed by a large pig,' Michael objected.

'Well, she's not squashed now,' Mrs Tucker said. 'She's enormous. I don't know what they did to her in Her Majesty's Prison for Bad Birds but she's almost as large as a pig herself. And take it from me; she's very gassy with it. That bird makes Mr Tucker's fart powder smell like a bunch of roses.' She shook her head ruefully. 'I should have realised something was up. Thomas tried to tell me.'

'Aye, youze should have sniffed it out, Edna,

what with yoouuurr training as a secret agent,' Mr Tucker remarked.

Atticus didn't think it was very fair of Mr Tucker to blame Mrs Tucker. Benjamin Posh-Scoundrel had fooled everyone, except himself, Mimi and Thomas of course! But then cats were much cleverer than humans at working things out.

'Yes, all right, Herman,' Mrs Tucker said. 'There's no need to go on about it. Anyway, on the second morning at dawn – a few days ago now – the whole beastly lot of them mounted an attack on us. At first we thought it was the deadly river creatures, but then we realised it was the Tofflys, Ribena, the Ambassador and those blasted birds. They rammed us with *The Toffly Treasure Hunter*, came aboard armed with pistols and chased us off the boat into the jungle.'

'I's come across some bloodthirsty pirates befoorrrre,' Mr Tucker said darkly, 'but I's never seen anything like them Tofflys when they're on the attack.'

'What happened then?' asked Michael.

'We waited until *The Toffly Treasure Hunter* had

left,' Mrs Tucker said. 'We thought we might be able to sail back upriver in *The Jolly Jellyfish* and raise the alarm. But when we returned we found they had taken Howard Toffly's journal, the map and most of our supplies.'

'The greedy gizzards took me giant parachute,' Mr Tucker growled. 'And me basher and me smasher and me squasher and me mini tarantula-bat repellent. The only thing they left was me faart powder and me beard-jumper shampoo.'

'That wasn't quite all, Herman,' Mrs Tucker corrected. 'Luckily they left the woolly-monkey suits too.' She continued the story. 'So there we were – at the mercy of the river creatures when night fell, with no means of defending ourselves and no food or water. That's when we realised the woolly monkeys were watching us. I thought maybe Nellie had foreseen that something like this might happen, which is why she knitted the onesies for us, so we slipped into them and waited. And sure enough, after a little while the monkeys came to the rescue.'

Atticus looked up. The monkeys were still there. A group of brown woolly faces stared at him curiously.

'They were very kind,' Mrs Tucker said. 'They looked after us. They showed us how to swing through the trees and sleep in the treetops and forage for food.'

'Nice swinging, by the way,' Atticus said to Thomas. 'I'm impressed.'

'Thanks,' Thomas said. 'It's all about balance. The monkeys use their tails, just like we do, except theirs are stronger. I'll show you if you like.'

'Maybe,' Atticus said cautiously. He wasn't keen on heights but he didn't want to sound like a wimp in front of Thomas.

'That's so cool!' Callie said. 'I wish I could learn how to swing through the trees.'

'I'm sure it's very easy when you get the hang of it.' Inspector Cheddar was bustling about pretending to do something.

'It's not *that* easy,' Mrs Tucker said.

'Especially if youze got a wooden leg,' Mr Tucker agreed. 'The monkeys had to give me a piggy back.'

'What did you eat?' asked Michael.

'Fruit mostly,' Mrs Tucker said.

'And bugs,' Mr Tucker added. 'I think I's got

some in me pockets.' He pulled out three enormous wriggling millipedes. He popped one in his mouth.

'Eeerrrrgggh!' said Callie.

'They's not that bad,' Mr Tucker said. 'Although they's keep getting stuck in me dentures.' He took his teeth out to show everyone. Bits of black millipede shell and quite a lot of legs nestled in the gums.

'It sounds like a real-life Tarzan adventure,' Callie said enviously.

'Ah-a-ah-a-ah-a-ah-a-ah!' Inspector Cheddar yelled.

The woolly monkeys shrieked back at him. One of them – a huge male – shook his fist at Inspector Cheddar and let out a tremendous scream.

'I'd back off if I were you,' Mrs Tucker told the Inspector. 'That's the leader. He thinks you're challenging him to a fight. He'll probably bite your head off. Now, let's get after those crooks. We'll take the amphibious vehicle.'

'What about me boat?' Mr Tucker sobbed.

'Get over it, Herman. There's a job to do. Bring what you can!'

A grumbling Mr Tucker thrust the fart powder

and the beard-jumper shampoo in his pockets
along with the millipedes.

'Hurry!'

Atticus glanced at the horizon. They had lost
track of the time while they were talking. Dusk
was gathering fast. The sun was sinking like a
stone. The woolly monkeys had fallen silent and
the river was an inky black.

Any minute now, the deadly river creatures
would attack.

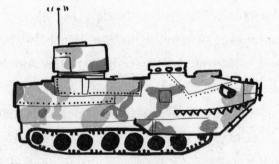

18

'I'll go first,' Inspector Cheddar said importantly. He leant over the rail of *The Jolly Jellyfish* and scratched his head. 'Hmm, I wonder where those logs came from?'

Atticus felt his hackles rise. There hadn't been any logs there when they'd crossed the gangplank to *The Jolly Jellyfish*: only mud. He pawed anxiously at Mrs Tucker.

'Oh, my giddy aunt!' she said. 'It's the crocodiles. They must have sneaked up on us while we were talking. Stand back, everyone!'

'Are you sure they're crocodiles?' Inspector Cheddar squinted down. 'They look like logs to me.' At that second the crinkled black snout of a huge crocodile thrust its way up between the boat's rails. SNAP! The crocodile twisted its head and snapped its jaws at Inspector Cheddar. Inspector Cheddar fainted. He toppled head first towards the mud. Mrs Tucker made a grab for his ankles. Somehow she managed to drag him to safety, away from the snapping crocodiles. 'Stay away from the edge of the boat!' she cried.

'What are we going to do, Mum?' Callie said in a small voice.

'Don't worry,' Mrs Cheddar said. 'We'll think of something.' She glanced at Atticus despairingly.

Atticus purred his understanding. The kids were in danger. It was his responsibility as the world's most cat-tastic cat to protect them. They had to get back across the gangplank to the amphibious vehicle before the other river creatures attacked. The Tofflys had taken all the bashing and smashing equipment but there was still something they could use to scare away the crocodiles. He dashed over to Mr Tucker, raised himself on to his hind legs and pawed at his pocket. (He didn't actually want to put his paw *into* Mr Tucker's pocket in case he got slimed by a millipede!)

'Me faaarrrrt powder!' Mr Tucker cried. 'Good

thinking, Atticus! That'll give 'em a pong in the snout.' Mr Tucker lay down on his tummy and wormed his way towards the rails. He raised the fart powder in his hand. Just then another crocodile snout appeared. This time the crocodile snapped at Mr Tucker. SCHWIP! 'It's after me beard-jumper!' he cried, wriggling backwards. 'I's can't get close enough.'

Now what? thought Atticus.

Suddenly a small, furry kitten shot through the air on the end of a vine. It grabbed the fart powder out of Mr Tucker's grasp and sprinkled it on the crocodile-infested mud. Then it landed lightly on the deck of the amphibious vehicle and grinned back at Atticus.

Thomas! Atticus didn't know whether to be cross or proud that the kitten had done something so dangerous. But it had worked. There was a small explosion as the fart powder combusted with the sticky mud to produce a super-strength pong. A cloud of eggy fog enveloped the two vessels.

'Head for the gangplank!' Mrs Tucker hoisted Inspector Cheddar on to her shoulders in a fireman's lift. 'Go!'

Mrs Cheddar went first, then Callie and Michael and Mrs Tucker with Inspector Cheddar on her back. Then Atticus and Bones. Everyone was coughing and spluttering. The smell was revolting. Atticus risked a glance down. The mud was heaving with the writhing, twisting bodies of crocodiles. They were heading back to the river as fast as their short little legs would take them. His plan had worked, with Thomas's help. Atticus decided not to be cross. The kitten had been incredibly brave.

Professor Verry-Clever threw open the door to the tank's attack-proof cabin. 'Quick!' he choked. 'Get in!' They tumbled inside one after another.

'You're okay!' Mimi curled her tail around Atticus's.

'Apart from being a bit smelly,' he said. He cleaned his whiskers quickly. 'Talking of which, where's Nellie?'

Mimi pointed through the galley to the sleeping quarters. 'She went to get some more wool from her bunk.'

'Oh.' *Stupid question*, thought Atticus, rubbing hard at his whiskers. *More to the point, where was Mr*

Tucker? Everyone was accounted for, apart from him. Atticus peeped out of the window. The cloud of fog had dispersed. *Oh no!* Mr Tucker had almost crossed the gangplank. His good leg was on the deck of the amphibious vehicle. But for some reason the wooden one wasn't. It seemed to have disappeared over the side.

'HELP!' Mr Tucker shouted. 'ME LEG'S STUCK!'

'Wait here!' Mrs Tucker threw Inspector Cheddar on to the sofa and rushed back outside to help her husband. She gripped Mr Tucker under the armpits and heaved. Mr Tucker's leg didn't budge. It was stuck between the amphibious vehicle and the gangplank.

Atticus tried to think what to do. It was pitch dark apart from the light in the cabin. His sharp ears heard the sound of gnashing teeth and swishing fish tails coming from behind the amphibious vehicle. There were flying piranha fish gathering at the edge of the river! If he didn't do something soon, Mr and Mrs Tucker would both be chewed to death.

Suddenly Atticus had an idea. The river creatures liked to attack under cover of darkness. But the Commander had said the amphibious vehicle could travel at night. *The headlights!* He leapt on to the instrument panel and searched for the switch. *FLICK!* All at once the river was bathed in light. The gnashing and swishing stopped. The flying piranha fish had swum away!

'Good work, Atticus!' Professor Verry-Clever congratulated him. 'That should do it.'

'Ouch!' Mr Tucker yelled. 'There's a leech in me trousers.'

Or not! The deadly river creatures weren't finished yet, thought Atticus. He'd have to come up with another plan.

'I can't do anything about that!' Mrs Tucker shouted at her husband. 'You'll just have to put up with it.'

'What about the anaconda round me waist?' Mr Tucker gasped, his eyes popping.

'Bloomin' hake!' Mrs Tucker jumped back. A huge snake had wrapped itself around Mr Tucker's arms and trunk. It was squeezing the life out of him.

Think! Atticus told himself. *Think!*

'Bones, help me get a rope round it and we'll try and pull it off!' Mrs Tucker ordered. 'The rest of you, try and find something slippery to free Mr Tucker's wooden leg!'

Callie and Michael searched through the cupboards with Mrs Cheddar and the Professor. 'There's nothing here,' Callie said.

But Atticus knew of something. His eyes gleamed. *Mr Tucker's beard-jumper shampoo! That was slippery!* He dashed out of the cabin. Mrs Tucker had lassoed the anaconda with Bones's help, but still the snake wasn't letting go.

'Aaarrrrggghhhhh!' Mr Tucker's face was purple. 'It's squishin' me!'

'Give me a hand!' Mrs Tucker shouted at the others. 'Make a line!'

'One, two three, HEAVE!' yelled Mrs Tucker,

wrapping the end of the rope around her waist. It was like a tug of war between the humans and the anaconda with Mrs Tucker as the anchor. So far though the snake was winning. It didn't budge.

Atticus dithered on the deck. He couldn't reach the beard-jumper shampoo in Mr Tucker's pocket unless the anaconda let go.

'Owwwwww!' Mr Tucker yelled. His face had gone from purple to blue and back to purple again.

Just then Nellie appeared at the cabin door. In one of her withered hands she held a long, knitted woollen snake. She threw it towards Atticus. The snake landed beside his front paws. He regarded her in puzzlement. *What was he supposed to do with that?*

She looked at him steadily. Then she said, *Stab it with your claws.*

Except this time Atticus was sure she didn't actually *say* it; not out loud anyway. Nellie hadn't opened her mouth. She was up to her witchy tricks again! She was talking to him in his head! He shook his head hard, his ears flapping, trying to get her out.

You heard me, Atticus. This time Nellie's voice was sharp. *Stab it!*

166

Atticus didn't dare disobey her. He bared his claws and pounced on the knitted snake. To his amazement, the real anaconda writhed and twisted. Whatever witchy thing he was doing, it seemed to be working.

Do it again.

Atticus pounced a second time. The anaconda let out a furious hiss. Atticus could see that its grip was loosening.

Now pull it off.

Atticus grabbed the tail of the knitted snake with his paws and gave it a sharp yank. This time the anaconda let go of Mr Tucker. It unravelled itself from his body as if a great force were pulling it, and disappeared over the side of the amphibious vehicle. There was a soft squelch as it landed in the mud.

'It's gone!' Mrs Tucker cried. 'Well done, everyone!'

Atticus felt dazed. No one else had seen what happened. Only he and Nellie knew why the snake had really let go. He wobbled unsteadily over to Mr Tucker, reached into his trouser pocket, took out the beard-shampoo and squirted it over Mr Tucker's wooden leg. He was so bewildered that he barely even noticed the millipedes scratching at his paw.

'Thanks, Atticus!' Mr Tucker's leg came free with a pop.

'Fall back, everyone!' Mrs Tucker ordered.

Atticus felt Callie scoop him up around the tummy. They stumbled into the cabin and slammed the door shut.

1·9

The following morning, approximately one hundred miles downriver, *The Toffly Treasure Hunter* was approaching the waterfall.

'Are you sure you've fixed the parachute on properly, Benjamin?' said Lady Toffly from her deck chair, where she was busy polishing a pair of gleaming pistols with SpoonBrite. Lady Toffly was still wearing her raiding-party outfit, which consisted of a camouflage suit, a pair of stout lace-up boots and a brown headscarf knotted beneath her chin like the one the Queen wears when she goes horse riding.

'Yes, Antonia, quite sure,' her son-in-law replied. 'I just need to pull the ripcord when we go over the cliff.'

'Well, have another look, would you?' Lady Toffly barked. 'I don't want to take any chances. Then get me my waterproof flak jacket from the cabin. There's a lot of spray up ahead.'

Benjamin Posh-Scoundrel ground his teeth. The goofy old bat was really getting on his nerves. Since she'd successfully led the raid on *The Jolly Jellyfish* three days ago, Lady Toffly had been acting like a modern-day queen of the ancient Maya, bossing him around like a doomed slave.

'And while you're down there, you can get me another pair of pistols to polish. And a large brandy. That champagne you brought is for sissies.'

'Very well, Antonia.' *Grind, grind, grind.* Benjamin Posh-Scoundrel told himself to stop. He wouldn't have any teeth left at this rate. It was lucky they were big, like the rest of him, or they'd be ground to stumps by now. He felt his shoulders sag. The truth was it wasn't just Lady Toffly's bossiness that was making him grind his molars like a demented ruminant. It was her belligerence. The Ambassador had never heard such a blood-curdling screech as when Lady Toffly had boarded *The Jolly Jellyfish* (not even in a film); nor witnessed such a determined advance on the enemy (in this case the Tuckers and their cats); nor anticipated such a thorough demolition job of the enemy's supplies. Lady Toffly hadn't even baulked at the repulsive stink coming from Mr Tucker's sock drawer. She'd just turned it out and grabbed Howard Toffly's papers without batting an eyelid.

Thus it was only now, having seen the resolute set of her horsy jaw, the steely glint in her gimlet eye, and the piratical curl of her upper lip, that Benjamin Posh-Scoundrel realised exactly what a tricky problem he faced. How, precisely, was he going to stop Lady Toffly from getting her mitts on the treasure? It was obvious from the raid on *The Jolly Jellyfish* that Lady Toffly would sooner shoot him than allow him to give any of the lost treasure of the jaguar gods back to the Nicaraguan government.

And if he didn't give any of the treasure back to the Nicaraguan government he would never become a lord.

Somehow, though, being a lord just didn't seem enough any more. Sailing along this river in the middle of the jungle in the paddle splashes of the ancient Maya made him yearn for something *more*. Imagine, he thought, what it must have been like a thousand years ago. Imagine the treasure. Imagine the slaves. Imagine the king. Imagine the sacrifices that had been made along the way to appease the jaguar gods. His mind went to the two sacrificial masks, which were still lying untouched in Howard Toffly's chest under the Ambassador's extra-large bed. His eyes sparkled.

Imagine the priests . . .

They were the ones with the real power. Just think: if *he* had been a priest of the ancient Maya, he could have had Lady Toffly sacrificed at the click of his fingers. Oh what joy to put on a sacrificial mask and point a priestly finger at the bossy bat; what satisfaction to see Antonia hauled up the steps of the Acropolis to the sacrificial slab; what delight to hear the crowds baying for her blood; what comfort to know that the tables were turned and that he was finally in charge . . .

'Benjamin, stop daydreaming!' shrieked Lady Toffly. 'We're nearly at the fall!'

The Toffly Treasure Hunter was picking up speed now. They were heading full tilt for the waterfall. From down below in the cabin came the sound of chattering magpies and a vomiting parrot.

BLLEEEERRRRRGGGGGHHHH.

Benjamin Posh-Scoundrel checked the parachute one last time. The river boiled and churned.

'Ribena! Roderick! Get up here at once!' Lady Toffly shouted. 'You're missing all the action. And bring my umbrella and a large brandy. Benjamin's useless. It's because he's not a lord, you know.'

'Yes, Mother.' Ribena and Lord Toffly emerged on deck and took their places beside Lady Toffly.

'What are you waiting for? Now, Benjamin! NOW!' screamed Lady Toffly, opening the umbrella.

His head still full of priestly whims, Benjamin Posh-Scoundrel pulled the ripcord. The parachute billowed above them.

The Toffly Treasure Hunter sailed straight over the cliff and began an elegant descent into the valley of the jaguar gods.

Two days later . . .

Back on the amphibious vehicle, Atticus had finally plucked up the courage to describe to Mimi what had happened the night Mr Tucker was attacked by the deadly river creatures. Since then, the rescuers had made good progress without further mishap. To his relief, Nellie hadn't tried anything else witchy. Atticus was beginning to wonder if he'd imagined the whole thing. 'It was as if I stuck my claws into the anaconda, not the knitted snake,' he told Mimi uncertainly. 'But I'm not sure now if it really happened or not.'

'It must have,' said Mimi. 'That snake wasn't

going anywhere and then it suddenly let go.'

'But why?' asked Atticus, bewildered. 'Or should I say *how*?'

'I think it's called voodoo,' Mimi said, frowning. 'It's a type of magic. The doll represents the person or creature that's doing you harm. Nellie must have knitted up the snake to save Mr Tucker, then used you to help her.'

'So I *am* her familiar, then?' Atticus said gloomily.

'It looks like it.'

'Why choose me, though?' Atticus asked sulkily. 'Why not Thomas, or Bones, or you?'

'Because you have the most power,' Mimi said. 'Your instinct is the strongest. You're related to an Egyptian cat pharaoh. You understand things we don't. Nellie's magic might not work with Thomas, or me, or Bones, or any of the cats at the cats' home for that matter. It can take years for a witch to find her familiar.'

Atticus sighed. It was all very well having instinct and knowing things without being told them, but he still didn't want to be a witch's cat. His tail sagged. Was that what Nellie had in mind when she said she'd come on the expedition in case they needed any knitting doing? That the two of them could do voodoo together?

Mimi read his expression. 'Don't worry,' she said soothingly. 'I'm sure Nellie would only ever ask you to help in an emergency. She'd never ask you to hurt anything unless there was no other choice.'

Atticus felt a bit better. It was true what Mimi said: if Nellie hadn't knitted the snake for him to pounce on, Mr Tucker would have been crushed to death by a large anaconda.

'Everyone on deck!' Mrs Tucker interrupted his thoughts. 'You've got to see this!'

Atticus and Mimi scampered up the steps from the cabin.

The river had widened into a great delta. Atticus could barely see the other side; it was so far away. And the current had picked up. The amphibious vehicle was keeping close to the bank but further out in the middle of the river the water eddied and swirled over rocks and boulders as if it was in a tearing hurry to get somewhere.

'Look!' meowed Mimi.

Ahead of them a vast cloud of mist hung in the air in a giant curtain. From beyond it there came a great booming and crashing sound.

The waterfall!

'We'd better get out of here,' Mrs Tucker said. She picked a spot on the bank and directed them towards it. The current was getting stronger. The amphibious vehicle was being borne along by it. Mrs Tucker fought with the controls. Eventually they reached the bank.

'Hit the TANK button,' Mrs Tucker instructed. Together Callie and Michael flipped the lever and the tank crawled out of the river on its tractor tyres and into the rainforest.

'We'll go through the jungle and see if we can find another way down to the lagoon,' Mrs Tucker said. She put the tank into gear. 'Hold on, everyone, I think we're in for a bumpy ride.'

They bumped along through the trees. Mrs Tucker had to keep swerving to avoid banging into the thick trunks. Atticus felt a bit sick.

'Excuse me, Mrs Tucker.' Inspector Cheddar lurched over. 'Don't you think we're getting a bit far away from where we want to be?'

Atticus groaned. Inspector Cheddar had his 'I'm in charge here' face on.

'Definitely not,' Mrs Tucker replied. 'I think we should go out wider so we don't fall off the cliff. Besides,' she added, pointing in the direction Inspector Cheddar wanted to go, 'the jungle's too thick that way. There's no knowing what might be lurking in the undergrowth.'

'Well, I used to be a traffic policeman,' Inspector Cheddar reminded her stiffly. 'So I think I should decide.'

There was a tense silence.

'Fine!' Mrs Tucker said eventually. 'Be my guest.'

'I've got a bad feeling about this,' Atticus said to Mimi.

'Me too,' she admitted.

Inspector Cheddar took the wheel and swung

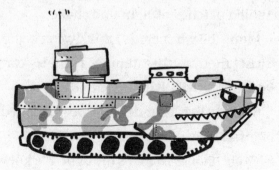

the tank to the right. They crashed through the vegetation. *Bumpety-bumpety-bump. Judder-judder-judder-judder-judder.* Atticus thought he was going to throw up.

The vehicle slowed to a crawl. The vegetation was thicker than ever. The jungle seemed to crowd in on them, as if it were trying to force the tank to a halt. Branches slapped at the windows and thumped on the roof. The ground was boggy and treacherous. Thick black mud splashed on the windows like treacle.

All of a sudden Atticus felt a familiar tingling sensation in his tail. Gradually it spread all the way through his fur, along his body, to the tips of his ears. They were in danger – real danger! He peered upwards through the tangle of green. His tail twitched. Something was moving up there in the dappled patches of light and shade.

'Mimi,' he whispered, 'I think we're being hunted.'

Just then a threatening rumble came from overhead. 'RRRRRRRRRRRRRRR!'

'Sounds like thunder,' Inspector Cheddar said cheerfully. 'I think it's going to rain.'

It's not thunder, Atticus thought. He knew exactly

what it was. So did everyone else, apart from Inspector Cheddar, come to that.

'Dad!' Michael whispered. 'It's not thunder.'

'What is it, then?' Inspector Cheddar said.

'It's a jaguar,' Professor Verry-Clever told him.

Something heavy dropped on to the roof of the cabin. THUMP!

'RRRRRRRRRRRRRR!' The rumble came again – this time from close above their heads. The vehicle shook.

'Don't panic!' Mrs Tucker said quietly. 'Everyone stay still. It's just having a look.'

'RRRRRRRRRRRRRR!'

The vehicle rocked slightly as the jaguar jumped off the roof.

'Where's it gone?' Inspector Cheddar stuck his face up against the window and peered out. At exactly the same moment the jaguar's face appeared on the other side of the glass and peered in. It eyeballed Inspector Cheddar. Then it opened its mouth and let out an earth-shattering roar.

"RRRRRRRRRRRRRRRRRRR
RRRRRRRRRRRRR!"

Atticus covered his ears with his paws. He had never heard anything as loud as that roar.

Jaguar spit splattered over the windscreen. Inspector Cheddar fainted again.

'Oh, for heaven's sake!' Mrs Tucker exclaimed. She picked the Inspector up and threw him back on the sofa. 'Stay still, everyone,' she repeated. 'It'll go away soon.'

'RRRRRRRRRRRRRR!'

Another rumble came from nearby. *There wasn't just one jaguar out there; there were two.*

'RRRRRRRRRRRRRR!'

Make that three! They were hunting in a pack, Atticus realised. Only jaguars didn't usually hunt in packs; they hunted alone. More jaguars surrounded the tank. Atticus counted four, five, six . . .

'There are seven of them, Mum!' Michael said.

Howard Toffly had seen seven jaguars. Could these be the same ones? Atticus rejected the idea as impossible. Howard Toffly's expedition to find the lost treasure of the jaguar gods was over a hundred years ago. He swallowed. *Unless these jaguars really were the jaguar gods of the ancient Maya.*

Atticus suddenly felt an overwhelming sense of

foreboding. It was like the feeling he'd had in the attic at Nellie Smellie's house only a thousand times worse. It screamed at him like an invisible police siren. DANGER! DANGER! DANGER! DANGER! His fur puffed out, his ears flattened against his head and his tail went rigid. It wasn't just the jaguars – gods or not – that they should be scared of. There was something else. He just knew it. They had to forget the treasure and leave now! He pawed frantically at Mrs Tucker.

'What is it, Atticus?' she said. 'What's the matter?'

'Meow, meow, meow!' he yowled.

Clickedy-clickedy-click. Nellie was still knitting. 'I think he's telling you to get out of here,' she said quietly. 'Fast.'

For once Atticus felt grateful to Nellie. Maybe the witch-cat bond wasn't such a bad thing, after all. At least Nellie could explain to the others what he was trying to tell them!

'Okay.' Mrs Tucker threw the gears into reverse. The tyres spun but they didn't move. The vehicle was stuck in the mud!

'RRRRRRRRRRRRRRR!'

The jaguars were closing in. Atticus felt the vehicle rock. They were trying to push it over!

'I'm sorry, Atticus, but there's nothing for it. We've got to go on.' Mrs Tucker put the tank into first gear and slammed her foot on the accelerator. The tank lurched forwards. The two jaguars in front of it jumped out of the way. The tank ploughed through the jungle. It was virtually impossible to see out of the window. It wasn't just the vegetation that made it difficult; it had begun to pour with rain. It was coming down thicker and faster than even the jaguar spit. Water streamed over the windows as if they were in a car wash. Only unlike a car wash, there was no let-up.

The tank slithered about. They were heading downhill now. And they were rapidly picking up speed.

'What's happening?' asked Mrs Cheddar.

'I've lost control,' Mrs Tucker said. She tried to slam on the brakes. 'I can't stop!'

The tank careered along.

'It's a mud slide!' shouted Michael. 'Hold on!'

All of a sudden the jungle dropped away. The

tank plunged over a precipice. They slid down the mountain on a torrent of mud. Atticus felt his stomach sink and churn. They were in freefall! He thought he might faint, like Inspector Cheddar. It seemed like forever until the tank finally levelled out and slid to a halt.

'Thank goodness for that,' Mrs Tucker panted. 'I thought we'd had it there for a minute.' She flicked on the windscreen wipers. 'Holy coley,' she whistled.

Atticus peeped out cautiously. They had arrived in the valley of the jaguar gods. It was exactly as Howard Toffly had described. The amphibious vehicle had come to rest a little way from the lagoon. Behind the lagoon crashed the waterfall. Behind the waterfall lay great caves. And from within the caves came the glint of piles and piles of twinkling precious stones. They had found the lost treasure of the jaguar gods.

But it wasn't the lagoon, or the waterfall, or the

caves or even the treasure that commanded their attention.

It was the sight of the army of warriors who had come to meet them.

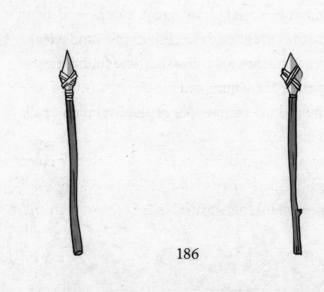

The warriors were clad in furry loincloths and boots. On their heads they wore feathered headdresses. They surrounded the amphibious vehicle and raised their spears.

'I think they want us to get out,' said Nellie, popping her knitting and a few other things into a bag. 'Come along.'

Atticus wondered how she could be so calm about it. The thought crossed his mind that she might have something *witchy* planned. But if she did, she was keeping it to herself. He couldn't pick up on it at all.

Everyone clambered out of the cabin, except Inspector Cheddar who had to be carried by Mrs Tucker because he was still in a faint from seeing the jaguars. They stood in a group, facing the warriors.

'I don't believe it!' Professor Verry-Clever scratched his great dome-shaped head. 'They're . . . they're . . .'

'ancient Maya,' Michael whispered.

'They didn't die out after all!' Callie's eyes were as big as saucers.

No, thought Atticus, *they didn't*. This was what he'd been dreading, without quite being able to put his paw on it. These warriors were the descendants of the king of Pikan and his followers. The jaguar gods hadn't killed them as Howard Toffly had assumed. Nor were the masks that Howard Toffly brought back with him relics from a thousand years ago. They were fresh. So was the skeleton he had seen. It had been put there by the Maya either as an offering to the jaguars, or some kind of grizzly warning for anyone who strayed too close to their secret world.

Amazing though it was, the ancient Maya had survived here, in the valley of the jaguar gods, hidden away from the modern world for a thousand years.

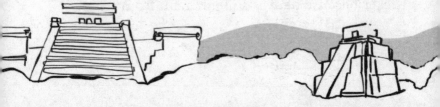

Inspector Cheddar had woken up again. He stared at the warriors. 'Who are they?' he asked.

'They're the ancient Maya, Dad,' Michael said.

'They didn't die out,' Callie explained.

Just then there was an ear-splitting squawk. The warriors moved apart to make a path, bowing low. A very large man with a very big head passed between them. He was dressed in a colourful tunic decorated with feathers and beads. Upon one of his very wide shoulders perched an enormous parrot.

'Posh-Scoundrel!' Professor Verry-Clever exclaimed.

'Professor Verry-Clever.' Benjamin Posh-Scoundrel didn't look at all pleased to see his old teacher. 'How *very* annoying of you to turn up. Just when I was beginning to enjoy myself.' He smiled smugly. 'What do you think of my discovery? The ancient Maya, eh? Who'd have thought it?'

'It's not your discovery,' Professor Verry-Clever said coldly.

'Yes, you cheated!' Michael said hotly.

Inspector Cheddar drew himself up. 'I'll deal with this.' He marched over to Benjamin Posh-Scoundrel. 'I have a warrant for your arrest,' he said, rattling a pair of shiny handcuffs at the Ambassador. 'And yours!' He found a slightly smaller pair for Pam.

'Beak it, copper!' Pam squawked.

Honestly, thought Atticus. Pam's language hadn't improved since her spell in Her Majesty's Prison for Bad Birds.

'Well said, Pam.' Benjamin Posh-Scoundrel raised his fist. In response the warriors lifted their spears. They started to chant and stamp with their feet.

'HUM! HUM! HUM! HUM! HUM! HUM!' The noise was deafening, like the jaguars' roar.

'Posh-Scoundrel seems to have some sort of power over them,' Professor Verry-Clever whispered. 'We need to be careful.'

'HUM! HUM! HUM! HUM! HUM! HUM!'

Benjamin Posh-Scoundrel held up his hand for silence. He addressed the warriors in a commanding

190

voice using a language Atticus had never heard before.

'What's he saying?' Mrs Tucker asked anxiously.

Professor Verry-Clever listened carefully. 'He says the Inspector is an evil spirit. He says he's come to take them to the underworld.'

'Oh dear,' said Mrs Cheddar.

Pam let out another squawk. 'CAT! CAT! CAT! CAT! CAT!' she shrieked, flapping at Atticus.

Atticus froze. *Pam had recognised him!*

Benjamin Posh-Scoundrel's gaze fixed on Atticus. 'So *you're* the cat detective,' he said. 'Ribena told me to watch out for you.' He addressed the warriors again.

'*Now* what's he saying?' asked Mrs Tucker.

'He says we're *all* spirits from the underworld, including the cats,' the Professor translated. 'He says we've come to steal their treasure and destroy their civilisation.'

'Hang on a minute!' Callie said indignantly. '*We're* not here to steal their treasure! It's Benjamin Posh-Scoundrel and the Tofflys they've got to look out for. Can't you tell them that, Professor Verry-Clever?'

'I'll try.' Professor Verry-Clever began to shout

191

in ancient Mayan over the din. No one took any notice of him. 'I think it might be my accent,' he said in a worried voice. 'I was never as good as Posh-Scoundrel at extinct languages.'

Benjamin Posh-Scoundrel barked out an order.

One group of warriors surrounded the humans. Another group surrounded the four cats. Atticus found himself looking at the sharp point of a spear. 'Don't,' he warned Thomas. The kitten was hissing and spitting. 'We'll have to wait until we get the chance to escape.'

'Why are they even listening to you, anyway?' Michael asked Benjamin Posh-Scoundrel defiantly.

'Because I know their culture and their language,' Benjamin Posh-Scoundrel answered. 'Because I appeared from nowhere on a boat which flew over a waterfall suspended from a giant parachute . . .'

'That was *my* parachute!' Mr Tucker cried. 'You thief!'

Benjamin Posh-Scoundrel ignored him. 'I also brought with me some gifts for the king. Or at least that's what I told him.'

'What gifts?' Mrs Tucker demanded.

'Three magpies, a parrot as big as a pig, two

elderly slaves and Ribena,' Benjamin Posh-Scoundrel replied with a smirk. 'Although I think I'll keep Pam as I've become rather fond of her.' He gave the parrot a bit of fruit from his pocket. Pam gobbled it up greedily.

'You've given your wife away!' Inspector Cheddar said, shocked. 'You fiend!'

'Well, I haven't exactly *given* her away,' Benjamin Posh-Scoundrel said. 'The king wants to marry her.'

'But Ribena looks like a cross between a warthog and a hippopotamus!' Michael whispered to Professor Verry-Clever. 'Why would the king want to marry *her*?'

'The ancient Maya have a different idea of beauty,' Professor Verry-Clever whispered back. 'It's entirely possible that to the king, Ribena is a vision of loveliness.'

Atticus found it hard to believe that *anyone* would think Ribena Posh-Scoundrel was a vision of loveliness, but if that's what the Professor said, he supposed he must be right.

Callie had been thinking about something else.

'What do you mean, two elderly slaves?' she demanded.

'Ribena's pestilential parents, of course.' Benjamin Posh-Scoundrel's eyes filled with malice. 'You're wrong about me wanting to steal the treasure. That was Lord and Lady Toffly's idea. And it was Ribena who suggested we should arrange a nasty surprise for the Tuckers so that her beastly parents could take back Toffly Hall. All *I* ever wanted was revenge on the Tofflys.'

Revenge? Atticus pricked up his ears. That's what the magpies wanted: on him! But why did Benjamin Posh-Scoundrel want revenge on his in-laws?

'I don't mind Roderick, but Antonia is a pain in the loincloth.' Benjamin Posh-Scoundrel scowled. 'You have no idea what I've had to put up with from that woman over the years. Nothing has ever been good enough for her: not my job as the British Ambassador to Nicaragua; not the fact that I can speak four hundred languages (three hundred of which are extinct); not the fact that I won an Olympic gold medal; not even the fact that I'm cleverer than Professor Verry-Clever.' He let out a deep sigh. 'And all because I'm not a *lord*.'

So that was it! Benjamin Posh-Scoundrel had a massive chip on his very wide shoulder.

'I planned to find the treasure, return it to the government of Nicaragua and claim all the glory,' the former Ambassador said.

'Aha!' said Professor Verry-Clever. 'I knew it.'

'I believed Her Majesty the Queen would make me into a lord and I could shut Antonia up once and for all by being grander than she was. Well, now I don't need Her Majesty's help. Thanks to my new friends here in the jungle, I'm *better* than a lord. I'm to become a prince of the ancient Maya. Ha, ha, ha!'

Atticus winced. Benjamin Posh-Scoundrel had gone into super-villain mode.

'My first thought was to ask the king to sacrifice Antonia to the jaguar gods,' Benjamin Posh-Scoundrel confessed. 'But then I realised even that was too good for her. Oh yes. Life as a slave is the ultimate comedown for Lady Antonia Toffly. She won't be so high and mighty when I've made her scrub Pam's poo bucket a few times. Not to mention the king's cesspit. I don't think anyone's pumped it out for nearly a thousand years.' He gave Pam another bit of fruit.

'BLEEEUUUURRRCHHHH!' Pam burped.

It probably wasn't a good idea to feed Pam too much fruit, Atticus thought. She might explode.

'You'll never get away with it,' Michael said.

'Who's going to stop me?'

'We will,' said Callie. 'Professor Verry-Clever will explain everything to the king. I'm sure *he'll* understand the Professor's accent. Then Dad and Atticus will arrest you and the king will set us free.'

'I don't think so,' Benjamin Posh-Scoundrel said. His eyes twinkled. 'Did I happen to mention that the king was so impressed by the sacrificial masks I brought with me, he has made me an honorary priest?'

There was a stunned silence. *An honorary priest?* Atticus was horrified. In the ancient Mayan world it was the priests who got to choose who should be sacrificed to the gods.

'So I get to choose who's sacrificed to the gods,' Benjamin Posh-Scoundrel confirmed. He pointed to Inspector Cheddar. 'And I say we start with you!'

'What?' Inspector Cheddar's eyes nearly popped out of his head. 'You can't do that!'

'I warned you!' It was Nellie who spoke. 'I warned you, but you didn't listen!'

It was true, thought Atticus. They should have believed Nellie. Bonkers or not, Inspector Cheddar *was* going to be sacrificed by the ancient Maya . . . unless Atticus could think of some way to save him. But for once in his nine lives he felt stumped.

Benjamin Posh-Scoundrel clapped his hands. The warriors raised their spears. 'To the Acropolis!' he shouted.

22

The city was in the thick of the jungle a short distance away from the lagoon.

It was an exact replica of the great city of Pikan. At its centre was the Acropolis, where the royal palace stood. Above the Acropolis a great stepped pyramid rose high into the sky. On top of the pyramid perched the altar where the priests performed sacrifices to the gods. And on top of the altar, Thug and Slasher had been set to work scrubbing the sacrificial stone.

'This is even worse than cleaning Pam's poo bucket!' Thug grumbled.

So far that morning the king had ordered the sacrifice of two chickens, one wife (to make way for

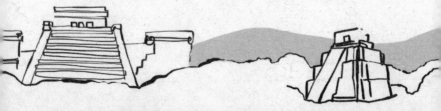

Ribena), seven slaves and a rat that had been found in the royal bedchamber; all to try to make it stop raining. Fortunately for the magpies it seemed that the jaguar gods were not appeased by the offerings: the rain had lashed down until lunchtime, taking most of the mess with it. Even so there was still quite a lot of sticky yukky stuff to come off.

'It's lucky we brought some spare Scrubbit,' Slasher grumbled.

'I don't see why we have to clean it anyway,' said Thug. 'The king's not fussed. The yuckier the better as far as he's concerned.'

'Benjamin Poshface persuaded him we should,' Slasher said. He clicked his beak angrily. 'Since he became a priest he's got even more hoity-toity than what he was when he was an ambassador.'

''Ere, Slash,' Thug said. 'Talking about Benjamin Posh-face, is it true about him giving Ribena to the king?'

'Yeah,' said Slasher. 'The king wants to marry

her so he's going to make Poshface a prince in exchange.'

'The king needs his eyes testing,' said Thug.

'You're right there, Thug,' Slasher shuddered. 'I'd rather marry Pam.'

'I wouldn't,' said Thug. 'I'd rather marry a packet of Scrubbit.' He mopped away at a stubborn bit of rat. 'Has Pam made up with the boss yet?' he asked.

'Nah,' Slasher said. 'She wants a divorce.'

'Does that mean she's still after half of our old nest under the pier?' Thug said indignantly.

'I s'pose,' Slasher said.

'Cos if she is that's not fair.' Thug felt unusually aggrieved. 'I mean, she's doing all right compared to us. She's sitting pretty, farting away and stuffing her gob with her new bessy, Benjamin La-di-da Stuck-up, while we're stuck here scrubbing this, that and the other . . .'

'Tell me about it,' Slasher said wearily.

'And if the king makes Posh-face a prince, think of all the treasure he'll be getting! I'll bet Posh-face gives some to Pam. He's practically in love with her.' Thug frowned. He was deeply troubled by the injustice of the situation. 'It's not right. I mean, if Pam can have half of our nest, why can't we have half of her treasure?'

Slasher regarded him in awe. 'Thug, me old mate,' he said, 'you're brilliant.'

'I am?' Thug said in surprise.

'Yeah, you're absolutely right. If Pam can have half of what Jimmy has, then Jimmy can have half of what Pam has! It's the law, innit?' Slasher slapped his friend on the back. 'Hey, Jimmy!' he shouted.

'What?' Jimmy Magpie snarled. He was busy sticking feathers to a mask with Pam's poo. He had to be very careful he didn't get it on his own feathers or *he'd* end up stuck to the mask. He hunched over the work with his back to the sacrificial slab, muttering bitterly to himself. 'Chaka-chaka-chaka-chaka-chaka!'

'Thug's had an idea!' Slasher said cheerfully.

'Well, here's one for him,' Jimmy said. 'Shut up and get back to work.'

'That's two actually!' Thug said with dignity.

'CHAKA-CHAKA-CHAKA-CHAKA-CHAKA!' Jimmy shouted at him.

Slasher and Thug exchanged looks.

This whole business with Pam and the Tofflys and being shut in a chest in a dark shed by Atticus Claw and then given away to a bloodthirsty king of the ancient Maya as a bird slave had really got to their leader. He seemed to have lost his appetite for shiny things.

'Nah, honest, Boss, it's a good one,' Slasher urged.

'Oh, all right,' Jimmy snapped. 'What is it?'

Slasher told him.

Jimmy's eyes grew round. Then they grew greedy. Finally they regained some of their old sparkle. 'That,' he said, 'is a very good point you make, Thug. Half of any treasure Pam gets from Prince Posh-face is mine – I mean ours – by rights.' He chuckled to himself. 'I'll go and tell the old crow now.'

He was just about to take off to find Pam when a loud squawk pierced the air.

'Talk of the devil,' he said, 'here she is.'

The three magpies watched as Benjamin Posh-Scoundrel led the procession up the steps of the temple to where the king sat on a great throne next to Ribena. Lord and Lady Toffly sat in front of them on three-legged stools, polishing the king's toenails with SpoonBrite.

The king shouted at the Tofflys to move. They shuffled to one side, bowing low. Lady Toffly's face was suffused with rage until she saw the prisoners, then it broke into an ugly smile.

'Likes a sacrifice, she does,' Slasher remarked. 'Cheers her up! Maybe that's what you need, Jimmy. A nice sacrifice to watch!'

The prisoners were pushed forward by the warriors and made to kneel in front of the king.

'Stone the crows!' Thug exclaimed. 'Look who it is!'

'It's Claw and his buddies!' Slasher gasped.

'Well, well, well,' Jimmy said. 'How the tables are turned! Perhaps you're right, Slasher. A good sacrifice might cheer me up after all!'

Thug regarded Atticus and the other cats ecstatically. '*Four* furry nest snugglers!' he said, clapping his wings together in delight. 'It's like Christmas!'

The three magpies flapped over for a better look. They were part of a much larger crowd. The arrival of the prisoners had got the whole city in uproar.

The king held up his hand for silence.

Benjamin Posh-Scoundrel spoke quickly to the king.

'What's he saying?' Thug asked.

'Search me,' said Slasher.

'Whatever it is, the king doesn't like it!' Jimmy chuckled.

The king was frothing at the mouth with anger. He gabbled something at Benjamin Posh-Scoundrel.

Benjamin Posh-Scoundrel nodded. He reached under his tunic and pulled out the jaguar mask.

'Ooh, look, he's putting on his sacrificial mask!' Thug said. 'I wonder who he'll choose first!'

Benjamin Posh-Scoundrel jabbed a finger at Inspector Cheddar. Two warriors grabbed Inspector Cheddar's arms and began to drag him towards the sacrificial slab.

'Ha, ha, ha! Inspector Cheese is first for the chop!' Jimmy sniggered.

Inspector Cheddar's body went limp.

'He's fainted!' Slasher said.

'What a spoilsport!' Thug remarked.

The warriors struggled with the Inspector's sagging body. The king looked on crossly. He started shouting again. The warriors dropped Inspector Cheddar on the steps of the temple.

'The king doesn't like it if they don't struggle,' Slasher commented. 'It's no fun. Prince Posh-face will have to choose someone else now.'

'I hope he chooses Claw!' Thug said.

Benjamin Posh-Scoundrel walked up and down the line of prisoners. He couldn't seem to make his mind up who to sacrifice next. He consulted Pam.

'PLAY! PLAY! PLAY! PLAY! PLAY! PLAY!' the parrot shrieked.

'What's she on about now?' Thug said.

'I think she's telling him to make the prisoners play the ball game,' Jimmy said.

'I didn't know she liked sport,' said Thug.

'She doesn't!' Jimmy said. 'She's the laziest parrot in the history of parrots. All she wants is to stuff her face with mango. They sell it at the game,' he explained. 'She went with Posh-face yesterday; she was gassier than ever when she got back.'

'What about the sacrifice?' Thug said anxiously. He was thinking about his nest snugglers.

'That happens when they lose,' Slasher said.

'What if they win?' Thug argued.

'They get to go free,' Slasher told him.

'They won't win,' Jimmy snapped. 'Trust me, they haven't got a chance. They're playing a team from the warriors. The warriors never lose. After the game they'll all get sacrificed together.'

'Hooray!' shouted Thug. 'I like games!' He frowned. 'Which team are we supporting?'

'The warriors, you moron,' Jimmy replied. 'Now let's get over to the court and grab ourselves some good seats.'

edge of the court. Atticus's eyes narrowed. *The magpies! Trust them to come and gloat!*

'Team talk!' Mrs Tucker said. They went into a huddle. 'We're only allowed seven players at once,' she said, 'so here's the starting line up.' She produced a scruffy bit of paper from her pocket. The team crowded round to see.

Mrs Tucker
Mrs Cheddar
Callie
Michael
Mr Tucker
Atticus
Thomas

'The rest of you are on the bench as substitutes. We need you to stay fresh and be ready to sub in at short notice. Okay?'

Everyone nodded, except Nellie, who was

already sitting on the bench, knitting, and Inspector Cheddar, who was still in a faint from nearly being sacrificed. They wouldn't be much good as substitutes, Atticus thought, but Mimi, Bones and Professor Verry-Clever would be up for it. Even so, he didn't rate their chances against the warriors.

'Now, here are the rules,' Professor Verry-Clever said. 'The object of the game is to get the ball into one of the hoops.'

'What hoops?' Atticus whispered to Mimi.

'Up there.' Mimi said, pointing to two stone hoops attached to the walls about halfway down the court.

'How are we supposed to do that?' Atticus said. The hoops were about five metres above the ground, near the top of the walls.

'Maybe you could throw it?' Mimi suggested. 'Like a netball?'

'You're not allowed to touch the ball with your hands or feet or paws,' Professor Verry-Clever was still explaining the rules.

Atticus and Mimi exchanged glances. 'No throwing, then,' Mimi said.

'Or kicking,' said Atticus despondently.

'What are we supposed to use?' Callie asked the Professor.

'Elbows, thighs, knees, bottoms, heads and, er, tails,' Professor Verry-Clever said. 'Any part of your body, really, as long as it's not your hands and feet.'

'What about me wooden leg?' Mr Tucker asked.

'I think that's allowed,' Professor Verry-Clever said uncertainly. 'I can't see why not.'

'How do you score?' Mrs Tucker said.

'The winner is the first team to get the ball through the hoop,' Professor Verry-Clever replied. He shrugged. 'And that's about it.'

It sounded easy enough, Atticus thought, except for the fact that the hoop was impossible to reach, they couldn't kick or handle the ball and they were facing a bunch of trained warriors who wanted them dead.

Nellie got off the bench and bustled over, her skirt rustling.

'I've knitted you some team bibs,' Nellie hissed. She glared at the warriors. 'They're made of spear-proof wool in case they try any funny business.'

'What sort of funny business?' Michael asked.

'Never you mind,' Nellie said. 'Just put it on.'

Atticus raised his eyebrows at Thomas. Nellie was in one of her 'do as you're told' moods.

They put on their bibs.

'How do I look?' Thomas grinned at Atticus.

'Great!' Atticus smiled back weakly. The kitten's excitement was undented despite everything. Atticus didn't want to be the one to tell him he was about to get flattened, like Pam had (except by warriors, not a large pig). He felt Mimi squeeze his paw. He knew what she was thinking: he had to set a good example to Thomas and the kids and act brave even if he didn't feel it.

'We'll nail them!' he meowed to Thomas. He hoped he sounded convincing.

You will with this, Nellie's voice echoed in his head.

Nellie was up to her witchy tricks again. Atticus regarded her with renewed hope. Maybe she had something else up her sleeve besides the bibs?

Nellie reached into her knitting bag and produced a small bottle.

Aha! thought Atticus.

'Gosh, Nellie,' Mrs Cheddar said admiringly, 'you really do think of everything!'

'Someone has to,' Nellie said. She rubbed some of the strengthener on Thomas's tail. It stood up, stiff as a brush. Thomas flexed it. 'It's like a woolly monkey's!' he purred in delight to the other cats.

'Your turn,' Nellie said to Atticus. He felt Nellie's hands on his tail. *PING!* Up went his tail in the air.

'Now you'll be able to hit the ball with it,' Nellie said. 'The ball's quite heavy, you know.'

SWISH! Atticus tried a few practice swings.

Just then a gong sounded for the start of the game.

'Let's do this!' Mrs Tucker punched her fist in the air.

'Good luck!' Mimi gave Atticus a kiss and scampered off the court to the substitutes' bench.

Atticus's mood had lifted. They were a great team! Mrs Tucker was pumped; Callie, Michael and Mrs Cheddar were fantastic at sport; and he and Thomas had super-strong tails. True, Mr Tucker was a bit of a worry on account of his wooden leg, but at least Inspector Cheddar wasn't playing so nothing could go seriously wrong. With Nellie's help, they might even win!

The referee threw the ball into the air. It was about the size of a football, but made of rubber.

Nellie was right – the ball was far too big and heavy for a cat to whack unless its tail was super-strong, like theirs. He was eager to give it a try.

The warriors charged towards the ball. One of them hit it with his elbow. It cannoned over to Callie, who managed to get her knee under it. Up it went again. One of the warriors stuck out a leg. It ricocheted off his thigh. Mrs Cheddar headed it. Another warrior struck it with his bottom. Mrs Tucker elbowed it. Mr Tucker tried to kick it with his wooden leg and fell over. The ball hit the ground, which meant that was the end of the point. The referee picked it up and threw it back up into the air. Off they went again.

This time Atticus got a swing at it. *SWISH! BASH!* It was a good strike. The ball sailed past one of the hoops, but it wasn't anywhere close to going through.

'Good work, Atticus!' Mrs Tucker shouted.

'Go, Jaguars!' Nellie and Professor Verry-Clever yelled from the bench.

Nellie had knitted up some pom-poms. Professor Verry-Clever, Mimi and Bones waved them enthusiastically.

The crowd booed. They wanted the warriors to win so that the prisoners could be sacrificed.

The next time Thomas got a shot. He thwacked it with his tail, like a baseball bat. The ball flew into the air and bounced off the wall near the hoop.

'Booooo!' yelled the crowd.

'Hurray!' shouted Nellie and Professor Verry-Clever. Mimi and Bones waved the pom-poms.

At the next break in play the captain of the warrior team called for a timeout.

The Littleton-on-Sea Jaguars returned to the bench and gulped thirstily at their water. The ball game was hot work, especially with Nellie's spear-proof bibs on.

'That tail strengthener is really working,' Mrs Tucker said to Thomas and Atticus. 'You just need to get the ball through the hoop.'

That was easier said than done, Atticus thought. 'We need to be closer,' he said to Thomas. 'We'll never score at this rate.'

Thomas squinted at the wall. 'How about I climb up to the top?' he said. 'If you can send the ball up, then I can hit it through.'

216

'Good idea,' said Nellie.

'What is?' asked Callie.

Atticus kept forgetting Nellie could understand Cat. Now she'd managed to tune into Thomas as well. At least she might be able to explain his idea to the others.

'Thomas is going to climb up the wall so he can get closer to the hoop,' Nellie said. 'All Atticus needs to do is tee it up for him and he can knock it through with his tail.'

'Like volleyball!' Callie said. 'Except with tails instead of hands!'

'That's a great idea,' Michael agreed.

Atticus wasn't sure. The wall was very high. What if Thomas fell off? But he didn't have time to say so. The gong went again. They were back on court.

24

In the posh seats at the front, Benjamin Posh-Scoundrel was watching proceedings with growing concern. The cats were much better than he thought they would be at the ball game. For some reason they seemed to have extra-strong tails since Nellie Smellie had rubbed lotion on to their fur. The king had noticed too. He was glued to the game. He kept pointing at Nellie and the two cats on court and jabbering excitedly about magic. More worryingly still, the king was also showing a strong interest in Mrs Tucker every time she charged at the ball, whooping and whistling his encouragement. It was almost as if he *fancied* her!

Benjamin Posh-Scoundrel's eyes narrowed. He'd sealed a deal with the king over Ribena. He didn't want the king to change his mind and marry Mrs Tucker instead, because then he'd never become a prince or be superior to Lady Toffly. The warriors had to win. They just had to. Then the rest of them – the cats, Nellie Smellie and Ribena's potential love rival, Mrs Tucker – would be sacrificed and that would be the end of that. He just hoped the warriors knew what they were doing. He scratched his head. It wasn't at all obvious how, if at all, he could help them.

He scratched Pam's chest lovingly while he tried to think of a plan. She was dreadfully bloated, poor thing. Rather like a barrage balloon. Perhaps he should put her on a diet when all this was over . . .

🐾

'You sure you'll be okay?' Atticus said to Thomas. The wall of the ball court towered above them. He didn't think *he* could climb it. But then he was afraid of heights and Thomas wasn't.

'I'll be fine,' Thomas said. 'The woolly monkeys taught me how to climb. I can get my paws in the cracks between the stones. My tail will help me balance.'

Atticus was still uncertain. It seemed an awful risk.

'Bones, come and sub in for Mr Tucker,' Mrs Tucker shouted.

Nellie rubbed Bones's tail with tail strengthener. Bones raced on to the court. The referee threw the ball in the air.

The warriors charged forwards again. Only this time they didn't go for the ball.

THUNK! A sandal-clad foot struck Atticus hard in the chest. Atticus rolled over and over in the dust. If it hadn't been for Nellie's spear-proof bib he would have been dead. Atticus picked himself up and did a cat stretch. He felt winded but he didn't think anything was broken.

'So you want to play dirty, then,' Mrs Tucker said to the warriors. She rolled up her sleeves and showed them her tattoo:

DON'T MESS WITH EDNA IF YOU WANT TO KEEP YOUR TEETH

'How about you pick on someone your own size!'

The warriors didn't pay any attention. This time

it was Bones they went for. One of the warriors stepped on her tail. Mrs Tucker shoved him off with a shoulder charge. 'They're trying to stop the cats!' she shouted. 'We need to close this out before one of them gets hurt.'

The referee started the game again. 'Let the warriors have the ball,' Mrs Tucker ordered. 'So they don't see Thomas climbing the wall.'

Atticus stood back from the game with Thomas while the warriors passed the ball from one to another. The others pretended to try and intercept. The crowd roared the warriors on. 'Now!' Atticus hissed.

Thomas ran to the wall and started to climb. The warriors didn't see him. They were trying to get themselves in a position to score.

'Hold off until he's out of reach of the warriors!' Mrs Tucker ordered the other players.

The warriors were working their way down the court. The ball was getting closer and closer to the hoop. *Elbow-knee-thigh. Elbow-knee-thigh.* They had a rhythm going now. It wouldn't be long until they scored. Atticus waited anxiously. The prisoners would have to be careful.

Thomas wriggled up the wall. Atticus watched him in amazement. He really did climb like a woolly monkey, especially now he had a strong tail to help him.

Elbow-knee-thigh. Elbow-knee-thigh. The warriors were underneath the hoop, getting ready to flick the ball through. The crowd was going wild.

Atticus gave a big wave with his tail. Thomas was out of reach.

'Okay!' Mrs Tucker said. 'Let's take them down.'

This time it was the Litttleton-on-Sea Jaguars who charged at the ball. The captain of the warriors saw them coming. He went for a shot on the hoop with his elbow. Mrs Tucker threw herself at him just in time. She grabbed him by the ankles in a rugby tackle and pulled him to the ground. The ball soared into the air, missing the hoop by a fraction.

'Oooooohhhhh,' roared the crowd.

Thomas had reached the top of the opposite wall. He crept towards the hoop, keeping low. But the crowd had seen him. Everyone started pointing. Benjamin Posh-Scoundrel was on his feet, shouting with Pam on his shoulder, screeching away.

'CAT! CAT! CAT! CAT! CAT! CAT!'

The warriors swung round. They looked up, bewildered.

'Get into some space, Atticus,' Mrs Tucker cried. 'We'll send you the ball.'

Atticus got into position beneath the hoop. 'Thomas, get ready!' he called. 'We'll only get one shot.'

'Oh no, you don't!' a posh voice bellowed. It was Benjamin Posh-Scoundrel. 'Pam, go get him!'

A large green balloon rose up from the crowd. It floated towards Thomas slowly, flapping a pair of wings. Atticus gasped. It wasn't a balloon; it was Pam! She was going to try and push Thomas off the wall!

'CAT! CAT! CAT! CAT! CAT! CAT! CAT!' shrieked Pam. She had nearly reached Thomas.

She lunged at him viciously with her beak. Thomas smacked her away with a paw. Pam floated about, flapping furiously.

'Peck him, Pam!' shouted Benjamin Posh-Scoundrel.

Come on, thought Atticus. *Get the ball!* But the warriors were back on the attack. The Littleton-on-Sea Jaguars couldn't shake them off.

'CAT! CAT! CAT! CAT! CAT!' Pam pecked at Thomas again. He wobbled on the top of the wall, his paws slithering this way and that on the slippery stone, using his tail for balance. Atticus watched helplessly. She was going to knock him off!

Mimi raced over. She had something between her teeth. She dropped it in front of Atticus. 'It's from Nellie,' she said.

Atticus dragged his eyes away from the battle on the wall and focused on the object at his feet. It was a round, green, knitted parrot. Nellie had knitted a voodoo doll of Pam! This time he didn't need Nellie to tell him what to do. He pinned the knitted parrot by the tail with his claws.

Pam let out a horrible squawk. But she wasn't finished yet. Her momentum carried her forwards. She bashed into Thomas with her huge, inflated body.

Atticus flexed the claws on his other paw. He didn't particularly like hurting anything, even Pam, but there was nothing else for it. He got ready to jab his claws into the knitted parrot.

'The ball, Atticus! Hit the ball!' Mrs Tucker shouted.

Atticus looked up. The Littleton-on-Sea Jaguars had found space. The ball was winging its way towards him. Instinctively he dropped the voodoo doll and swung at the oncoming ball. *SWISH! THUMP!* It came vertically off his tail and soared up towards the top of the wall.

Thomas flexed his tail, ready to strike the ball through the hoop.

'Don't, Thomas!' Atticus shouted. He could see that the kitten needed his tail to balance while he fended Pam off. If he hit the ball he would fall. 'Save yourself!'

Pam flapped towards Thomas, beak gaping.

Atticus pounced on the voodoo doll and sunk his claws into it.

'THTTHTTTHTHTHTHTHTH!'

Pam didn't exactly pop. Instead, all the gas that had been building up inside her fizzed out of the punctures that had been made by Atticus's claws.

'I'll be okay now!' Thomas shouted down. 'She's had it!' He swung at the ball with his tail. It sailed through the hoop. *They had won!* But neither Thomas nor Atticus had reckoned on Pam's flatulence. The parrot was out of control, like a

balloon with all the air escaping, except much, much, much heavier and full of fruit gas. She cannoned into Thomas like a small meteor. Then she whizzed backwards and forwards over the court before landing in a cascade of parrot poo on top of the magpies.

PLOP!

'CHAKA-CHAKA-CHAKA-CHAKA-CHAKA!'

But Atticus couldn't care less about the magpies. Or Pam. All he cared about was Thomas. 'Hang on, Thomas!' he meowed desperately. 'Hang on!' Thomas was still trying to cling on to the wall with his front paws but the force of Pam's impact was so great that even his monkey tail couldn't save him. The kitten lost his grip. He fell through the air and landed on the ball court with a dull thud.

25

'Thomas!' Atticus raced over to where the kitten lay.

Thomas smiled at him weakly. 'We did it!' he whispered. Then he let out a long shuddering breath and closed his eyes.

'Thomas!' cried the children.

'I'm afraid he's very badly hurt, children,' Mrs Tucker said quietly, gently stroking the kitten's limp body.

'He'll be all right, though, won't he?' Callie was crying. So was Michael.

'I don't know.' Mrs Cheddar hugged them close. 'Poor Thomas!'

'He saved our lives!' Professor Verry-Clever sniffed.

'He's me favourite kitten!' Mr Tucker sobbed. 'Come on, Thomas, wake up!' Tears streamed down his beard-jumper and dripped on to the court.

Atticus stroked Thomas's ears. Mimi and Bones were beside him. 'Atticus,' Mimi began, but he turned away. This was his fault. He shouldn't have been such a scaredy-cat. He should have climbed the wall, not let Thomas do it. And he should have finished Pam off by throttling her when he'd had the chance. As it was, Pam was still alive and Thomas was seriously injured. He might not even survive! Thomas was only a kitten. He had eight more lives to live! But he had risked them all at once to save his friends.

He heard the rustle of skirts. Nellie knelt beside him. 'Don't worry,' she said to the children. 'I thought something like this might happen.' She reached into her knitting bag and drew out a small tube. 'That's why I brought some spare ointment. He'll be fine in a minute.'

228

Atticus felt a glimmer of hope. If anyone could help Thomas, Nellie could. Nellie took the lid off. To his surprise she offered the tube to him.

You do it, Atticus, said her voice in his head. *The magic is stronger when a witch and her cat work together.*

So he *was* her familiar. It was definite now. Nellie had said so. Atticus gazed at Thomas with his big green eyes. He wasn't going to fight it any more. He just hoped that Nellie's faith in him was justified.

Give me your paw.

He allowed Nellie to squeeze some ointment out of the tube on to his paw.

Now rub it under his chin.

Very gently, Atticus rubbed the ointment into the fur under Thomas's chin with soft strokes of his paw. 'Come on, Thomas,' he purred gently. 'Come on!' He felt Thomas stir. It was working! Atticus rubbed a bit more ointment in.

Thomas lifted his head. Then he sat up. 'That tickles!' he said. Then he saw the humans. 'What's the big deal?' he asked Atticus. 'Why is everyone looking at me?'

Atticus didn't get a chance to reply.

'He's okay!' Michael cried, scooping Thomas up.

'Oh, Thomas!' Callie buried her face in his fur. 'We were so worried!'

'That ointment really works, Nellie!' Mrs Cheddar said admiringly.

'You can stop crying now, Herman!' Mrs Tucker told her husband. 'Thomas is fine.'

'Thomas!' Mr Tucker blew his nose on his beard-jumper. He stroked the kitten in delight.

Atticus couldn't have felt happier if he'd eaten a whole basket of sardines. He didn't mind that Thomas was getting all the attention. Thomas was all right. He and Nellie had cured him. Not that anyone else would realise that, or quite how close Thomas had come to death, except Mimi, of course. Everyone else just thought that Nellie's ointment was a bit magic, like her, and that Thomas had had a bad bump. They didn't know anything about Atticus being Nellie's familiar or how he made Nellie's magic more powerful or how they'd made Pam pop with the voodoo doll.

And that was how he wanted it to stay.

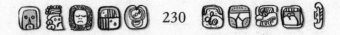

230

Just then there was a great hullabaloo amongst the crowd.

'The king is coming!' Professor Verry-Clever said.

The king waddled over, accompanied by his courtiers, Benjamin Posh-Scoundrel and Ribena amongst them. The former Ambassador to Nicaragua looked furious. Atticus crossed his paws. Hopefully now they'd won the ball game, the king would listen to Professor Verry-Clever, even if he did have a funny accent. They were heroes, after all!

The defeated warriors fell at the king's feet. He kicked them out of the way. Atticus felt a bit sorry for them. According to the rules, the losers would have to be sacrificed, unless Professor Verry-Clever could persuade the king to spare them.

Benjamin Posh-Scoundrel opened his mouth to say something but the king silenced him with a dirty look. He went up to Callie and squinted hard at Thomas.

Thomas purred uncertainly.

The king said something to his courtiers.

'His Majesty says it's a miracle that Thomas is still

alive,' Professor Verry-Clever translated. 'He says that Nellie's ointment must be magic and wonders if he could have some for his toothache.' The king approached Nellie. To everyone's amazement he fell on his knees in front of her. 'He says he would be honoured if you would become his new priest.'

'But *I'm* his priest!' Benjamin Posh-Scoundrel protested.

The king said something else.

Benjamin Posh-Scoundrel gasped in dismay.

'What's he saying?' asked Michael.

'He's telling him not any more, you're not, sunshine,' Professor Verry-Clever told them. 'He's saying he obviously doesn't know anything about being a priest and that he's probably just a cheap lowlife crook who's taken him for a ride. He's also saying he'd rather eat a pile of beetle dung than marry Ribena, because she's probably in on it too.'

Ribena started crying.

'And as for the elderly slaves, he wants

to get rid of them immediately because that's the worst toenail polish he's ever had.'

'Bravo!' said Mrs Tucker.

Mrs Tucker was looking a bit sweaty what with the ball game, the heat and the spear-proof bib, Atticus thought, but the king really seemed to like her despite all that. It must be something to do with him having a different idea of beauty, he supposed. Atticus watched in some trepidation as the king sidled over to Mrs Tucker, beaming. The king muttered a few more words.

'And as he doesn't want to marry Ribena any more he would like to marry Mrs Tucker instead.'

'In your dreams!' Mrs Tucker muttered. She drew herself up. 'Tell the king I am very honoured by his offer but I'm already married to Herman here –' she waved a hand at Mr Tucker – 'and in our country the Queen does not allow us to have more than one husband at once.'

Professor Verry-Clever translated. The king

looked disappointed. He frowned hard at Mr Tucker as if he was thinking about sacrificing him. Then he noticed Mr Tucker's beard-jumper. The king seemed quite intrigued. He went over to examine it.

'Tell him also that Nellie will give him her magic ointment to cure his toothache if he lets us return to our own people in our amphibious vehicle. And that Herman will show him how to grow a great beard-jumper of his own,' said Mrs Tucker. 'And tell him we would like to take the false priest, his wife, the elderly slaves, the magpies and what's left of the parrot that was once the size of a pig with us back to the United Kingdom so that they may be punished for trying to trick him.'

Professor Verry-Clever explained all this to the king.

He nodded his agreement.

'Oh, and one last thing,' Mrs Tucker said. 'Tell him that the warriors shouldn't be sacrificed for losing the ball game, as it was partly Nellie's magic that made us win.'

The king thought for a moment before he

nodded again. A great cheer went up from the warriors. The king waddled back to his throne with Nellie, who proceeded to show him how to rub the ointment into his gums.

Just then Inspector Cheddar woke up from his faint.

'Dad!' Callie and Michael ran over to the bench. 'You'll never guess what happened.' They told him all about the ball game and about Thomas falling off the wall and being cured by Nellie's ointment.

'You should have used that ointment on your tooth, Dad! Callie said. 'It really works. Look at the king. He's feeling better already!'

The king was showing Nellie a war dance. He looked as happy as a flea.

'Ha, ha!' Inspector Cheddar said. 'Very funny! I expect Thomas was just pretending. Well done for winning the ball game, though. Pity I didn't get to play or we'd have scored much sooner. You should have woken me up.' He pottered off to retrieve his handcuffs from the warriors.

Atticus watched him fondly. Inspector Cheddar had *sort of* got there in the end, he supposed. Although he'd missed most of the action and

nearly caused them all to be sacrificed, he would at least get to arrest the villains.

Another shout went up from the warriors. They crowded round Thomas, hoisted him on to the captain's shoulders and ran round the court, cheering. They were giving him a lap of honour. Normally Atticus felt a bit jealous when Thomas got all the attention but not this time. He didn't mind a bit. Thomas deserved it.

'Are you okay?' It was Mimi.

'Yes,' he said.

'You did a great job,' she said. 'Congratulations.'

'Thanks.' There was just one small thing that was still troubling him, though. 'Er, Mimi,' he said. 'You know how Thomas stowed away on *The Jolly Jellyfish* and lived with the woolly monkeys and climbed up the wall just now and everything . . .'

'Yes.'

'Well –' it was hard to know how to put this – 'you don't think I'm getting *boring*, do you?'

Mimi laughed. 'You, boring?' she said, twining her tail around his. 'Don't be silly. You're full of surprises. And you have the most cat-tastic adventures in the world.'

Atticus felt relieved. He wasn't quite ready to hand over to Thomas yet, although he thought he might be one day. He purred contentedly. It was good to know that for now, anyway, he was still the world's greatest cat detective.

Buckingham Palace
London

Atticus Grammaticus Cattypuss Claw Esq.
                    2 Blossom Crescent
                    Littleton-on-Sea

Dear Atticus,

I am writing to thank you and your
friends for your excellent work in
Nicaragua. I was delighted to hear that
the ancient Maya didn't die out after
all but I was also very cross to learn
that my former Ambassador, Benjamin Posh-

Scoundrel, turned out to be a complete
scumbag. To think that he intended to
claim all the glory for finding the lost
treasure of the jaguar gods so that I
would make him a lord! He's a disgrace to
our great nation. I hope the judge sends
him to prison and throws away the key.

Professor Verry-Clever (for whom I have
the highest regard) tells me that Posh-
Scoundrel's wife, Ribena, is not much
better. I expect she'll get a spell in
the clink with her parents, the magpies
and that detestable parrot. Let's hope
it teaches them a lesson. Going round
trying to steal the king's treasure
indeed! The cheek of it! And the king
seems such a nice person. He sent me
a lovely letter in hieroglyphs, which
Professor Verry-Clever translated,
asking if I'd like to go and stay with
him. I said I'd think about it. To be
honest I'm not sure about the journey
- I don't want those poisonous frogs

hopping into my royal pants. Anyway,
I said I'd see and if not, he should
definitely come and stay with me,
although he'll need to bring some proper
clothes as I hear that his loincloth is
somewhat scanty for the English weather.

The good news is the king is absolutely
thrilled with the Old Hag's Cure-All
Ointment that Nellie gave him. He's been
rubbing it on his tooth, like Nellie
showed him, and it's feeling much better
and he's not foaming at the mouth any
more. (Pity you couldn't persuade dear
Inspector Cheddar to use it!) To think
that's why the king was so grumpy all
that time and no one knew. No wonder he
sacrificed so many people — the poor man
was in agony. He says he hasn't felt
like sacrificing anyone in ages now, so
that's excellent news. His beard-jumper
is coming on famously as well thanks to
Mr Tucker's good advice and the jumper
Nellie knitted for him before she left.

Personally I'm very pleased that the
Nicaraguan government has declared the
valley of the jaguar gods a protected
zone so that the ancient Maya can
carry on with their traditional way of
life (apart from the sacrificing, let's
hope) and the jaguar gods (if that's
what they are) will be safe in their
caves. The king has agreed to lend the
treasure to a museum in Managua so that
other people can go and look at it,
but he wants it back soon otherwise he
thinks the jaguars will get annoyed
as they like guarding it. It's a very
sensible solution if you ask me. The
best way to secure the future is to
preserve the past. But you know that
because you're related to an ancient
Egyptian cat pharaoh!

With very best wishes,
Elizabeth
HRH Her Majesty Queen Elizabeth II

'*Atticus Claw Breaks the Law* is
now one of my all-time favourite
books. It is un-put-down-able.'
Helen, age 10

Atticus Claw is
a masterpiece!'
Sam, age 12

'Very funny
and interesting.'
Ara, age 9